HOPE

Coeur du Bayou Trilogy
Book Two

LISA COOTS

This is a work of fiction. Names, characters, businesses, places, events and incidents are either the products of the author's imagination or used in a fictitious manner.

Any resemblance to actual persons, living or dead, or actual events is purely coincidental.

Solunapublishing.com

P.O. Box 775
Jennings, LA 70546

ISBN: 0990766926
ISBN-13: 978-0-9907669-2-6

Cover Art: Phycel Designs, Inc.
phycel.com
Photo Credit: Sandylynn Photography
Duson, LA

DEDICATION

To my Sun and my Stars,
my reasons for living,
and to my parents,
who gave me
so many happy memories
to draw from.
I love you!

LISA COOTS

ACKNOWLEDGMENTS

Special thanks to Amy LeBlue for allowing me
to use her name, Natalie Manuel for offering
to wash my dishes so I could write faster, and
Sandylynn Photography for taking the
perfect picture for my cover. Also, to all of
my family and friends for keeping me
motivated by asking,
"Where's that second book at?"
Thank you for your support!
It means the world to me.
Special thanks to my husband, Dwayne Coots,
for allowing me to use one of his songs
as part of Faith and Jake's story.
I feel like it was meant for them.

LISA COOTS

HOME

A familiar sense of darkness
tugging gently at my soul.
Recognition flickers, then fades
too fast to name.
Something from the past
came alive through the music.
Enigma haunting my soul.
Can't leave it alone, it's too late.
Too late to turn back.
Slipping ever so slowly
until the darkness engulfs my soul.
Thought I could handle the madness
It's too late, too late to fight.
Just let go.
Tears of relief.
The darkness is comforting and
there's peace in my soul.
At last, I'm home.

Lisa Ardoin Coots
May 20th, 1991

CHAPTER 1

"Oh, Faith. It's beautiful!" Margaret exclaimed from somewhere over Faith's shoulder. She had once thought her mother's kitchen was huge, but trying to bake and decorate a cake in it had greatly diminished its size to borderline claustrophobic.

"Thanks, Mom." Faith sighed, stepping back to look at the cake from a different angle nearly bumping into her mother. The bottom tier was decorated like a tree stump, the top was a camouflaged wrapped gift completed with a pink shiny bow. Happy with her work, Faith turned the cake again. *Was that an air bubble in the fondant?* Groaning she rubbed a hand across her face unknowingly leaving a trail of powdered sugar. "Damn it."

"Faith Ann," her mother warned.

"Ugh. The kids aren't even here."

"It doesn't matter. Ladies don't swear," Margaret chided her.

"Mom, please. I've got to get this delivered before I pick the kids up from school," Faith said leaning closer to inspect the bulging lump that seemed to be growing before her eyes. "Besides, I've heard you say worse, right here in this kitchen."

"What? I don't remember that."

"Oh, yes ma'am. I have never seen you so angry." Faith searched through the utensils scattered across the table.

"I think you're mistaken," her mother snapped.

"No, you can ask Evan. He was there. Actually it was his fault." Faith poked at the offending lump with a toothpick, then smoothed the fondant gently with her fingertips. Her older brother, Evan, had always been there annoying and teasing her. She quickly learned to give as good as she got. Even now as adults the teasing continued.

"I have no idea what you're talking about," Margaret said dismissively. "Can I start cleaning up this mess now?"

"Remember, you had made a cake for Nonc Henry and Aunt Pie's anniversary. We were getting ready to leave. Evan was chasing me..." Faith finally turned to look at her mother. By the expression on her face, Faith could tell she was remembering. Red blotches grew on her cheeks and her eyes glazed over. " ...with a baseball," Faith finished then let the memory hang, suddenly sorry she brought it up.

"I worked so hard on that cake," her mother muttered miserably.

"I know Mom. I'm sorry. Why do you think I don't allow the kids in the kitchen when I'm making a cake for someone else?"

Margaret shaking her head, turned to the sink with a mixing bowl and began to scrub furiously.

"Ugh. I'm never going to make it," Faith grumbled glancing at the faded rooster clock on the wall. It had been hanging in the same place as long as Faith could remember. If it were ever removed, she knew there'd be an outline of it on the wall behind it.

"You want me to go pick up the kids?" her mother offered.

"No, I'll call Claire. Maybe they can just ride home with her. I'll never get it all done and make it to work on time." Knowing she was leaving the mess for her mother to clean made her feel guilty enough.

The winter had been harsh in more ways than one. The bitter cold and uncommon ice and snow had her feeling boxed in. She had taken a job at the diner and baked cakes on the side from her mom's kitchen.

Her mother's kitchen. Her earliest memory took place right here in this room. She was probably three or four wandering into the kitchen, awakened by a dream. The sound of metal pans and the smell of baking cake pulled her into the warm kitchen to find her mother who had comforted her and rocked her back to sleep with sweeter dreams. Faith smiled remembering, knowing full well she had come home for the same reason. She needed her family to comfort her after her failed marriage and this kitchen was where they gathered. No matter who was in the house, they ended up in the kitchen. Probably because there was always something simmering or baking in it. She had learned to bake in this kitchen standing on a step stool next to her mother. The worn wood cabinets and faded Formica countertop had been there longer than she had. Another fixture was the antique oven. Faith had no idea how old it was, but it was as finicky as a spoiled house cat, and also the reason she was running late.

Besides the two tiered birthday cake, she had six pies for the diner. Her boss, Gil, had agreed to buy the desserts she baked at home. It gave her more time to be at home with her kids. Tonight, however, she had the evening shift. Not her favorite this time of the year. The bright lights and heat from the kitchen kept her mind off of the cold gloomy weather outside and visiting with the customers kept a smile on her face even when she really didn't feel like smiling. She tried to not lose hope, but this winter and her pending divorce had just about dried it all up.

"I'll call Claire," Margaret suggested from the sink. "I know she won't mind. That way I can get this cleaned up and start supper."

"Sorry, Mom." Faith joined her mom at the sink bringing her cake utensils to be washed. Another familiar spot bringing back a flood of memories. How many hours had she spent at this sink, washing dishes, peeling potatoes or the like? A sudden flash of her at the sink, holding her hand under the cold stream of water to wash out a cut from a broken glass. She still had the scar.

"I didn't mean to leave you with this mess, but your oven put me late. You really need a new one. I wish you would have let us buy you one for Christmas."

Christmas. The word brought on another stream of memories. The pine smell of Christmas trees, presents, dressing up in brand new clothes for church and the itchy stockings that kept her fidgeting throughout the mass.

"My oven is fine. You just have to know how to use it." Her mother's voice brought her back.

Faith and her brother, Evan, had planned to surprise Margaret with a new oven for Christmas. The surprise was spoiled when Hannah, her nine year old daughter, had unintentionally spilled the beans before they could make the purchase. Margaret had forbid them to spend so much money on her and still insisted her oven worked fine.

"Thanks, Mom."

Sliding the cake slowly into the box, Faith held her breath only letting it out when the cake was safely in. Nothing had moved. She sighed with relief.

"Make sure they do their homework. No TV or video games till it's done."

"Faith Ann, I raised three kids," her mother reminded her.

"Yeah Mom, and look how great we turned out," Faith said rolling her eyes.

"Y'all turned out just fine."

"I guess we were perfect angels. Did you think that when we wrecked your cake?" Faith asked without thinking.

"No, y'all weren't perfect." Margaret's face reddened again.

"Especially Evan," Faith teased, grabbing the pies first, she headed for the door.

"Just go before you're late and don't forget your jacket."

"Sure," Faith answered automatically making her way outside. The cold fresh air was a nice contrast from the heat inside. After placing the pies in her car, she went back inside for the cake.

Checking the rooster clock again, she figured she just might make it. With her purse slung over her shoulder, she gently lifted the cake box and said a quick prayer she would get it there in one piece.

"Bye, Mom," she said as her mother held the door open for her.

Carefully placing each foot on the icy cement she walked slowly, holding her breath all the way to her car. Once she had the cake safely tucked in the back seat, she breathed in deeply.

Spring would come soon. She could smell it. It was there, dancing around the edges of these gray days. The sun had actually made an appearance today and stayed out for a few hours. Patches of clover were starting to sprout among the dead brown grass of her father's well-kept lawn. She longed for the green of the new grass and the colorful flowers that were waiting to bloom. Faith had been watching closely for signs of spring, as if its return would also signal the return of her hope. It was there, too. She could also feel it dancing around the edges of her sadness, like the sprouting buds waiting to break free.

CHAPTER 2

Faith sucked in a deep breath, realizing she had stopped breathing several blocks back. Her old neighborhood inched by at less than half the posted speed limit, and not for sentimental reasons. Every bump in the road had her checking the rearview mirror trying to see if the cake had moved. She could feel a tension headache building from the ping ponging her eyes were doing between the road and the mirror. She just knew her next glance back would bring her worst fear, to look back and see the top cake sliding off of the bottom one like some kind of Charlie and the Chocolate Factory landslide.

She hated this part. Delivering the cake was nerve-racking, but Faith couldn't trust anyone else to handle the cakes. If she screwed it up or tripped, it would be on her. She wouldn't be able to blame anyone else.

Forcing herself to breathe again, she turned off of the highway. Why did they have to live out here on a dirt road? A lady from town had ordered the cake, but it was for her granddaughter's birthday. The nasty winter weather had left the dirt roads badly rutted and in need of grating. As the car vibrated on the uneven surface, she glanced from the mirror to the clock on her dashboard. The original plan had been to have it delivered by noon, but her mother's oven had set her back a few hours. Now she'd be lucky to get it there before school let out.

Thankfully Claire, her brother's girlfriend that lived next door, was also Hannah's teacher. She'd be happy to give the kids a ride home from school. Shaking her head, she thought about Evan and Claire. Her lunkheaded brother was dragging his feet. She had fully expected a marriage proposal at Christmas. It didn't happen. Then New Year's. Nope. Surely, she had thought by Valentine's. Mardi Gras had even come and gone. Evan still hadn't proposed to Claire.

A loud pop and sudden jolt to her car had her slamming on the brakes. Gripping the steering wheel, she peered in the mirror at the cake, afraid of what she might see. It looked fine from where she was sitting. *Breathe. Breathe.*

The angle the car was sitting at let her know it was the tire. This was not happening. Praying she was wrong as she got out of the car, she let out a stream of curses when she saw she had been right. It was tempting to kick the tire, but she knew it wouldn't help.

Faith took in her surroundings and saw nothing but fields. No houses. Of course it had to happen out in the middle of nowhere with no one around. Tears of frustration formed as she sat back in her car to get her phone. She'd call her dad or Evan. *Calm down and just Breathe.* A few minutes late wouldn't be the end of the world. Digging through her purse she tried to calm herself.

Where was it? Don't panic. Breathe. Breathe. She chanted to herself as she thought back to that morning. A tear slid from her eye as she remembered slipping the phone into her jacket pocket. The jacket her mother had told her to bring. The jacket that was still hanging by the kitchen door. Damn it.

Now it was certain she'd be late delivering the cake and late for work. She had no way to let anyone know. This was unacceptable. She was never late. When she said she would do something, she did it.

"*Breathe.* You can do this." She pulled the lever to pop the trunk. "It's just a flat."

Muttering to herself, she walked around the back of her car. Argh. She had forgotten all the stuff in her trunk. Stuff she didn't need every day but hated to put in storage. Mostly photo albums and pictures. There wasn't any extra storage space at her parents'. The room she shared with Hannah was filled with Hannah's toys and things. Faith didn't have the heart to pack any of it away.

Somewhere under all of this was the jack and spare tire, if she remembered right. As she stood there trying to decide the best way to get at it without putting her precious photo albums on the muddy ground, she heard a vehicle approach.

"Yes, yes, yes. Help has arrived," she muttered excitedly poking her head around the side of the open trunk lid. Not recognizing the truck, she hid behind the lid again. Should she accept help from a stranger, or send them on their way? It wasn't in her nature to be needy, but time was an issue. Wrestling with looking capable or needy she decided on a compromise, casually helpless.

"Hey, Faith. You ok?" The familiar voice wiped all the arguments from her mind. It was none other than the one person she had been trying to avoid since she moved back to Cypress Point. Jake Fusilier. *Breathe.*

"Thank God! I was hoping someone would come along," Faith blurted without thinking.

"Well, I'm so glad to be the answer to your prayers," Jake gave her a sly wink then added, "It's really good to see you, Faith."

Faith couldn't help the eye roll, but answered truthfully. "It's good to see you, too."

Jake just laughed and got out of his truck. The years had definitely been kind to him. Yes, he had aged some, but she could still see the boy he had once been. At one time, he had been her brother's best friend. Two peas in pod. Jake being a lighter version of her brother, in coloring and attitude. Evan was dark and serious. Jake was more laid back and loved to laugh. He reminded her of the sun.

"You can sit in my truck if you're cold. You probably should have a jacket on. It's getting colder, you know." His eyes roamed over her, and she felt a flush on her cheeks.

"Yeah...." She sighed remembering her mother's words, then the cake. "No, I need you to take me to deliver this cake."

"What about the tire?" he asked perplexed.

"I can have Evan come to see about this later. Right now, I need to get this cake delivered. Then I need to get to work." Slamming the trunk closed she turned back to him. "Please."

"Sure." Jake shrugged, his brown eyes twinkling. "Let me help you with that."

"I'll get the cake. You open the door for me," Faith barked out orders, hurrying to get the cake.

"Yes ma'am." He chuckled as he opened the back door for her while she maneuvered the cake from her back seat.

"Oh, and grab these pies. They're for work."

Gently she slid the cake box into the back seat of his truck then turned to take the pies from him. Their hands brushed. *Breathe.* He smiled down at her. *Breathe.* She quickly put the pie boxes on the back floorboard and ran back to her car to retrieve her purse. *Shit. Shit. Shit.* Why did it have to be him? Why couldn't it have been some friendly farmer? Oh, wait. That was him, with that lopsided shit eating grin and those eyes, the color of melted chocolate. His caramel colored hair needed a cut. She had liked it long. If it grew out a little more just over his ears it would start to curl, the ends a lighter shade from the sun. The sun. Bittersweet memories flooded through her. Jake without a shirt, his skin tanned from working in the sun. *Breathe. Breathe.* She locked up her car.

"So where are we taking the cake?" Jake watched her as she got in the truck, the smile still on his face. She knew he was remembering too.

"Mrs. McMillian ordered a cake for her granddaughter's birthday."

"You made that?" he asked turning to look at it again.

"Yeah, why?"

"That's really cool." Giving her that lopsided grin again he added, "I remember. You did like to bake."

"I just need to get the cake there in one piece, ok?" Memory lane was not on her schedule for today.

"Bossy, too." He chuckled. "Yes, ma'am."

The bumpy dirt road was in desperate need of a grating to smooth it out. Every bump and jiggle had Faith clenching her teeth and looking into the back seat.

"You ok?"

"What?" she asked not taking her eyes off of the cake.

"If you're so worried about it maybe you should have just held it on your lap."

"No, it's better off on a flat surface." She forced herself to look out the window. "You know where she lives, right?"

"Yeah, out here, I know where everybody lives."

The rest of the drive was spent in silence. Faith was bombarded with memories of these dirt roads and Jake. She didn't need this right now.

As soon as he stopped the truck in front of the trailer home, Faith jumped out to get the cake. By the time she rounded the truck, Jake had gotten out and opened the back door for her.

As she reached for the box, she let out a small cry.

"What's wrong?" Jake peered over her shoulder, the heat from his body warming her back.

"The bow. One of the curly ribbons broke off," she said lifting it off of the cake gently, doing her best to ignore his nearness.

"No one will notice that. It looks great."

"I can't believe this," Faith said trying to hold back the tears. "Maybe I can fix it."

"Here. Let me." Jake grabbed the pink curly ribbon and shoved it in the cake near the base of the bow.

"No!" she cried too late.

"Look. It's fine. Problem solved. We make a great team, Faith." He smiled down at her with that lopsided grin of his.

Faith forgot to remind herself to breathe. "You.....Why? Don't.. touch.....cake....idiot," she stammered gasping for air. Hot angry tears gathered in the corner of her dark eyes.

Jake watched her with amusement then chuckled. "Faith, calm down. Everything is fine."

"I... am... fine."

"Take a deep breath, babe," he said rubbing her arms. "Just let it out."

She breathed deeply and let it out.

"You son of a bitch. You don't get to just show up and ruin my cake. I worked so freaking hard on that, and you just jabbed that....." she stopped to gulp more air. A tear rolled softly down her cheek leaving a trail in the smudge of powdered sugar.

Reaching out, he wiped it away then licked his finger and grinned at her. "Mmmm. You were always a perfect mix of spicy and sweet. I never minded the heat because it always made the sweet part sweeter."

Breathe. Breathe. Glaring at him, she turned back to get the cake.

"Hey Jake! What are you doing here?" a female voice called from the doorway of the trailer.

"Hey Tracey. You know me, helping a damsel in distress, making a cake delivery. Just a normal day." He winked at Faith as she carefully lifted the box and made her way to the door.

"Don't touch me or my cake again," Faith said through clenched teeth as she passed him. He immediately started to hum a song that he teased her with in high school. She froze for a second, and she could hear him singing softly.

"I guess it would be nice, if I could touch your body. Not everybody has a body like you."

Not waiting for the tagline, she walked straight up the steps to the door.

"Look at that! It's gorgeous! This is so awesome. Jade's not going to let me cut it," Tracey exclaimed.

"Where should I put it?" Faith smiled at her uncomfortably.

"Oh, just put it on the table." Dismissing Faith, she turned her attention back to Jake who had followed Faith halfway to the house. "So, Jade is having friends over, but later I could meet you for a drink, if you want."

"Nah, I'm not drinking tonight. Need to get some rest."

Faith didn't need to see Jake's face, she could hear the guilt in his voice. However, she could see Tracey and the blonde was literally licking her lips.

"I need to get to work. Enjoy the cake," Faith said pleasantly as she passed Tracey in the doorway again. Jake took the hint and headed back to the truck.

"Yeah, Mom paid you, right?" Tracey asked nervously.

"Yes, she did. Tell her I said thank you and tell Jade happy birthday for me." Faith didn't stop walking until she was back at the truck. Opening the door, she looked back at Tracey who was still eyeing Jake hungrily.

"I still can't believe you have an 18 year old," Faith called to her and waved before slamming the door of the truck.

Jake was still chuckling a half mile down the road.

"What are you laughing at?" Still perturbed, Faith gave him a sidelong glance.

"Faith, I'm so glad you came home. You haven't changed a bit."

Narrowing her dark eyes at him, she forced herself to take a breath before answering him. "Yes, I have. That was a whole lifetime ago. I'm not the same person."

"Whatever you say, babe."

"Don't call me that." Looking away uncomfortably she couldn't help herself, even though she didn't want to know the answer, "So, you and the bimbo have a thing?"

"Well, now. Why do you want to know?" he teased.

"Never mind. I was just curious." Faith looked back out at the fields.

"It's not like that." His voice was suddenly serious. "Faith?"

"I don't care who you see."

"Yes, I know you don't care or you say you don't." He shook his head at her. "I don't believe it. Not for a minute."

Breathe. The sudden serious turn had her chanting to herself again. *Breathe.* "Jake stop. I'm not having this conversation. I need to get to work."

"One day you're going to have to explain to me what happened to make you stop caring." His brown eyes held her gaze expectantly.

"Please..." she whispered turning back to the window.

The ride back to town was completed in heavy and uncomfortable silence. Faith felt miserable but she could not and would not go there. The past could stay where it was.

As soon as Jake stopped in front of the diner, Faith jumped out. Turning back to look at him, she gave him a small smile.

"Thanks for saving me," she said softly before she closed the door and ran into the diner without looking back.

CHAPTER 3

Jake watched Faith walk away, and cursed himself for caring. Being around her had triggered more than a flood of memories, his body remembered the feel of her and longed for more. The womanly curve of her hips and fuller breasts combined with the ponytail somehow made her even more sexier than the younger version. With one last swish of her ponytail, and sway of her jean clad backside, Faith disappeared into the diner.

Faith had left him and Cypress Point behind years ago. He kept telling himself the only reason she moved back was because of the divorce. But she was here. She came back. Part of him hoped he had something to do with it.

He considered again as he turned off the ignition, then grabbed the pies she had left in her rush to get away from him. It wasn't like her to forget things. She was usually the one that was so together.

Walking into the diner, Jake waved hello to Gil, the owner, and watched as Faith rubbed at the sugar on her face.

"You forgot these." He placed the pies on the counter, his voice all business.

"Oh. Sorry, thanks." Slipping an apron over her head she looked up in surprise. "Today has been crazy."

"Yeah, I get that." Not able to stay mad, he smiled at her. "Give me your keys and I'll go see about your car."

"You don't have to do that. I was gonna call Evan." She closed her eyes and sighed. "But I forgot my phone at home."

This was not the Faith he remembered. The Faith he knew didn't need to be saved, but he was glad to be the one to save her. "Just give me your keys. I know where it is. It's just a flat. I'll change it for you."

"You don't have to do that." Fidgeting with the tie to her apron, she looked down at her feet.

"I know I don't. I'm not in the habit of leaving people stranded."

"I can call my dad." Faith shrugged nervously.

"Your dad doesn't need to be out there in the mud, and he doesn't like driving after dark. Keys." He held out an open hand, not willing to take no for an answer.

"Ok, fine." Faith turned to the kitchen to retrieve her keys.

"Jake, you eating?" Gil asked through the opening to the kitchen. "I can throw a steak on the grill for you."

"Nah, I'll be back later though." He smiled easily thinking about Faith serving him.

She returned slapping the keys down in a huff, then she picked them back up and held them out to him. "I really appreciate all of this."

"I know," he said simply then wrapped his hand around hers. Jake heard her intake of breath, as he felt the tingle of desire grow with their touching skin.

Biting down on her lip, Faith looked down at their hands. "I owe you one." Snatching her hand away and grabbing a pie box she held it out to him. "How about a pie?"

"Hey, that's tonight's desserts!" Gil called from the kitchen obviously eavesdropping.

"It's ok. Keep the pie. I'll think of something." Jake looked away innocently and started humming a few notes of the song he had teased her with earlier.

"You'd better take the pie, Jake, or you'll end up with nothing," she snorted.

"See ya', Faith." He winked at her then headed back out to his truck, humming the whole way.

Driving through town, like always, he thought about Faith. There wasn't a place here that didn't remind him of her. Just about all of the memories he had of this town, included Faith; the countless football games, hanging out at the diner, joyriding in his truck, and kissing her goodnight on her momma's front porch.

When she had left for college, those memories kept him hoping for the day she would come home. He would be there waiting. News of her engagement had nearly killed him. It was supposed to be him, not some fake ass, fast talking yuppie. He had drowned the hurt and disappointment with drink and hanging out at the bars. He loved music and played a little. The music helped soothe what the drink couldn't numb.

Pulling up to her car, he smiled again. Faith was home, and she was free. He had been waiting a long time for this. He had kept his distance at first, not wanting to push and allowing her time to get things sorted out.

Halloween night had been an unexpected reunion, and not the one he had hoped for. Seeing her at the Halloween Festival with her friends, he had wanted to say hello, but she had disappeared in a hurry. Then later when everyone had gathered to search for Claire during the storm, Faith had showed up. He had followed her when she ran off into the woods after Evan and the dog. Jake had heard her screams, held her as she cried in the mud for her friend, and brought her back to the house. With all the chaos and their rush to get to the hospital, he wasn't even sure if Faith knew he had been there.

Opening her trunk, he cursed at the boxes in his way. Then noticing a framed picture, he pulled it out of the box. A family picture. He sucked in a breath at the instant pain that shot through his gut. There she was, the love of his life, smiling into the camera surrounded by her family. Her family with another man. Damn. It should have been him.

Knowing he shouldn't, but not being able to help himself, he opened up a photo album and flipped through the pages. All of the years of him wondering what she was up to, was answered. Pages of pictures of her wedding, birthdays, pregnancies and births. Her smiling face changing very little over the years. It hurt, but he kept flipping. Somewhere in the pages, he noticed her eyes had changed. She was smiling but her dark eyes told him she wasn't happy. There were more pictures of the kids and less of her and the jackass together. He didn't know what to think about that or how to feel. Happy. Angry. Empty.

Darkness was falling. He sighed, carefully putting the albums back in the box. Not wanting to put them on the muddy ground, he carried them all to his truck until he could get the flat changed.

Shining his headlights on her car, he made quick work of getting the spare on. Thinking to himself, and humming. She was here now, and there was hope.

"I gotta have Faith....Faith.....Faith."

CHAPTER 4

Ding. Ding. Ding.

The harsh ping of the order up bell cut through the noisy clatter of the diner, interrupting Faith's thoughts. Seeing Jake had opened the floodgates and she was having trouble closing them again. Too many memories at once.

"Order up!" Gil called through the order window, slamming his hand on the bell. *Ding. Ding. Ding.*

"Got it." Faith snatched the bell from under his hand.

"What are you doing?" Gil blinked at her, his hand frozen in midair.

"If you ring that bell again I'm going to bounce it off your nose." Faith gave him a wicked smile holding the bell just out of his reach.

"Hey, I don't know what's with you today, but I don't need this abuse." Gil sniffed loudly as he turned away from her, pretending to be hurt.

Faith cracked a smile at his obvious attempt at humor. Remembering the first time she had met the skinny boy with the shaggy blonde hair and buck teeth, she giggled to herself. Gil had dared her to walk the train tracks all the way to the bayou and back. Taking his dare, and then issuing it right back to him, he had no choice but to go with her. The dangerous part was not knowing when a train would come. When she thought of it now, she cringed. She hoped her kids would never be so foolish. They had completed the dare safely, but the return trip was spurred into a footrace by a surprise encounter with a water moccasin. Faith had never ran so fast in her life. She wasn't sure how she beat Gil back, his legs being twice as long as hers. Collapsing by their bikes in a fit of laughter, lungs burning, and friends looking on in admiration, they became friends. Remaining friends, even through the awkward pre-teen stages of acne and crushes, they had lost touch after she left for college. When she had returned to Cypress Point last fall, she was thrilled to learn he had bought the diner.

"You know you love me, and you can't stay mad," stating the obvious, Faith put a hand on her hip, "Besides, I make the best pies."

"Put my bell back and bring that order out. Then maybe I'll forgive you."

"Gosh, what is this a restaurant or something?" Grinning she put the bell back and picked up the food. She was still laughing when the bell over the door jingled. Glancing over and seeing Jake in the doorway, she nearly dropped the tray of food. Damn. How could it be after all of these years the sight of him still short circuited her brain? *Breathe. Breathe.*

"Have a seat, and I'll be right with you."

"Ok, I'll be at the counter."

Somehow she managed to serve the food without messing anything up. She could feel his eyes on her and fought the urge to look back at him. When she did turn, Gil was grinning through the order window wiggling his eyebrows and nodding toward Jake. Faith gave him a death glare making him duck back into the kitchen.

Rounding the counter, she realized Jake had caught the whole exchange.

"So what can I get you?" Focusing on what needed to be done, she hoped her hands weren't shaking.

"Ummm... let's see. The special looks good tonight. What do you think?"

"It ain't my mama's pot roast, but it's ok." Faith said loudly, knowing Gil was listening.

"Hey, I heard that," Gil called from the kitchen.

"It must be that time of the month. He's real sensitive today," she whispered loudly, giving Jake a wink.

"Faith, don't make me call your mama," Gil threatened, poking his head out of the order window.

"Ok. Ok. Truce." Faith held up her hands in surrender.

"The special is fine with me and I'm sure it's wonderful." Jake put her keys out on the counter in front of her. "You're all fixed up by the way."

"My knight in shining armor." The thought was out of her mouth before she finished thinking it. "I owe you. Supper is on me and I'll even throw in the pie."

"You don't have to do that."

"Yes, I do." Reaching for her keys, she made the mistake of looking into his eyes. *Breathe.*

"Ok, fine." He shrugged, grinning at her. "I'll stick around to give you a ride to your car."

"I can call someone." Faith looked away, not ready to be alone with him again so soon.

"I'm already here. No argument." Jake slapped a hand on the counter.

Faith let out a snort, turning back towards the kitchen so fast it sent her ponytail flying. Gil was waiting for her on the other side of the swinging door.

"What?" she snapped.

"Nothing. I'm just cooking, filling orders..." He shrugged his shoulders innocently.

"Good." Grabbing a knife she sliced the pie, crunching down when she got to the crust with forceful jabs.

"So that's it?" Gil's voice was curious and low.

"What's it?" She plopped a piece of pie onto a plate without looking up.

"You and Jake. That's why you're so moody today."

Faith turned on him, knife in hand flinging pieces of pie in his direction. "There is no me and Jake. I had a flat. He gave me a ride and helped me deliver a cake. It's been a rotten day. That's why I'm moody."

"Ok, Faith. Here." He held out the special. Snatching the plate out of his hand, she huffed out a breath and turned back for the pie. "It's just, you know, everyone remembers you and him."

"What?" Her trip down memory lane continued. She had tried for years to put Jake Fusilier out of her mind, only to come home and be reminded of him at every turn.

"Just that y'all dated and everyone thought y'all would end up together. I just thought maybe..." The glare she sent him stopped him from voicing those thoughts out loud.

"I'm giving him his food then I'm taking a break."

Walking back through the swinging doors, she carried Jake's order and placed it in front of him. Without saying a word, she placed the service set up next to his plate and simply walked out the door.

The sun was gone, and the cold air made her shiver. Breathing deep, she closed her eyes and willed herself to be calm. Everyone thought she had it all together. She had at one time, been so efficient, effective and in control. In the past few years something had changed. Maybe when she realized she had no control over her life. Things happened. Plans didn't always work out. Marriages either. Having children had been the greatest blessing, but was also her undoing. Miss Control Freak realized that she could not control the future. They were growing up, whether she liked it or not. She could only be there for guidance. At some point she would not be able to protect them. That scared her shitless.

The divorce, even though she wanted it, was an added stress and an unknown. She had come home to what she knew. Her family. Hoping to get back some sort of control, or at least a sense of normal.

Her feet felt slippery on the frozen sidewalk as she walked carefully pacing, rubbing her frozen arms against the chilly air. Sometimes she felt like if she didn't keep moving she would just fall down.

Jake. She had done her best to avoid him since she came back. Halloween night couldn't have been helped. Claire had been missing and everyone had shown up to search the woods behind Serena's house. Seeing her brother holding the unconscious Claire, she had all but fell apart. She remembered screaming and falling to her knees on the muddy ground, not being able to stand with the weight of the shock. Then arms holding her. Shouts and lights. Most of it a blur. Then just those strong arms holding her, a familiar voice telling her everything would be alright. Broken and sobbing, she clung on to him and the words she so desperately needed to hear. Jake had quietly held her, with just a beam of light in the mud, and let her release all of the tension and uncertainty. She had forgotten about those arms, but they felt like home. Home, where she felt safe and secure.

The bell over the door jingled, bringing her back to the present. Her knight in shining armor stood in the doorway.

"Hey, you need my coat? You're gonna freeze."

"No, I'm going back in. I just needed some air."

"Ok, I'll wait inside." Jake gave her that lopsided grin and disappeared back inside, leaving her in the dark with the muffled sound of the bell.

CHAPTER 5

"She ain't here."

"What?" Jake looked up from his plate to find Gil eyeing him.

"She ain't' here. It's her day off. I hope she's baking though. Those pies are long gone with that lunch rush we had today." Wiping his hands on his apron Gil's eyes wandered over to the empty glass display case.

"I came to eat, fool," Jake said using his fork to point at his plate.

"Yeah, ok. What's going on with you two anyway?" Gil leaned casually on the counter.

"What are you talking about? I've been eating here since you took over." Jake scooped up another forkful of rice and gravy.

"Yeah, until she started working here. Suddenly, you stopped coming. Now you're back after bringing her to work and picking her up. I'm not stupid." His green eyes narrowed at Jake.

"Hmm." Jake rolled his eyes. "That's a matter of opinion." When Gil kept staring at him, he continued, "She had a flat yesterday. She needed a ride. I stopped coming here because your menu has been the same. I need a variety. You know, change it up?" He circled his fork in the air.

"Please, my menu is still the same and you order the same damn thing every time. The only thing different is Faith, and her desserts." Crossing his arms over his chest, Gil waited for a response.

Jake pointed a finger at Gil, then touched it to his nose. "Bingo!" he said with a mouthful.

"Yeah, you can say it's the sweets, but I think you're sweet on her. Still."

"What's it to you?" Sitting up straighter, Jake put his fork down. Faith's friendship with Gil had never been an issue. Jake had never been intimidated by the scrawny kid, but that scrawny kid had grown into a man. A man that spent a lot of time with Faith, and seemed to be overly interested in his intentions.

"Oh, no. Nothing like that. Faith is a good friend. She's had a rough patch lately and I just don't want her to get hurt. That's all." Gil uncrossed his arms to explain using hands.

"Hurt? You mean the divorce?" Jake sat back in his chair. He had been happy to hear of her divorce, but had never considered how painful it had been for her.

"Yeah, she's having a hard time adjusting I think. She laughs and jokes, but I think it's mostly to hide the hurt." Gil's green eyes, now thoughtful, gazed out the diner window.

Jake blinked. "Wow. That's pretty deep coming from a short order cook, Gil. I had no idea you were such a sensitive soul." He grinned across the counter.

"Fuck off, Jake. I don't want to see her get hurt again." His tone now serious, Gil leaned forward, his hands resting on the counter in front of Jake.

"What makes you think I would hurt her?" Not liking this turn of conversation, Jake looked down at his half empty plate.

"The way she was all jumpy yesterday. That's not like her at all. You had her jumping at her own shadow."

"She just had a bad day. The flat, the cake, kids, work."

"No, I've seen her frazzled before. This was different. You still matter to her, so you could hurt her."

Offended by the accusation, Jake leaned forward shortening the space between them. "I'd never hurt her."

"Not on purpose, but admit it. You got a string of women waiting on you anytime you want. Big music guy. You're like a low rent rock star. My guess, that's because of her." Unflinching, Gil's gaze pinned him, his words missing the nerves and striking the bone.

"More sage wisdom from the king of the grill?" No longer hungry, Jake pushed his plate away.

"Hey, I only speak the truth my friend."

Without looking at him, Jake threw money on the counter, and flipped Gil off on his way out the door.

Jake was still fuming as he drove out of town, back to the wide open fields. He breathed in the fresh air. The scent of grass and dirt filled his nostrils calming him. The acres of soil before him would soon sprout into fields of rice. To him there was nothing prettier than the green of new rice under a brilliant blue sky. This is where he belonged. He never had any doubts about that. Third generation farmer. It was definitely in his blood. He loved the land as much as he loved music. Whereas the music flowed through him, the land grounded him and gave him peace. He was connected to it.

What did Gil know? Everything apparently. He had gone there looking for Faith, hoping to see her again. He had drove her back to her car and even followed her home to make sure nothing else happened. They laughed and joked like old friends. He wanted to ask her out, but she was finally starting to relax around him. He could wait. He wasn't going anywhere and he sure hoped she wasn't.

He kept thinking of the photo albums in the trunk of her car and all of the years he had missed. What did he have to show for those years? Hard work in the fields, sure. Money in the bank. Lots of nights in the bars. Lots of mornings hungover and waking up to strange women. While it had been mostly fun, he realized somewhere in the last few years that he was lonely. He had never thought much about the why of it. Gil was right. He played music and drank because he was hiding, too. Hiding from the fact that Faith had hurt him, and killed any hope of them being together when she had married that asshole.

Jake cursed to himself as the back end of the truck skidded out from behind him. He slowed, realizing he had been on the gravel road for a while. Just as the town held memories of him and Faith, so did the old back roads. He smiled remembering this very road led to one of their favorite meeting spots. An old barn, long forgotten, but still standing. He came here sometimes when he was feeling sentimental.

As he got closer, he caught a flash of light reflecting off of something near the barn. A car. He recognized the light blue sedan. Faith. What was she doing out here? Was it magic? Had he wished for her, and she appeared? Was she remembering too? The all-knowing Gil had thought she still had feelings for him. As much as Gil had pissed him off, he hoped he was right.

Shutting his truck door softly, he walked around her car noticing the new tire. Good, she had it changed. He knew her dad wouldn't let her forget about it.

The beams of sunlight shone through the cracks in the old weathered boards, casting shadows in the dusty air. Spring was definitely pushing its way through the winter days. Faith was sitting on the ground, her back against a support beam, eyes closed.

"Hey Faith," he said softly trying not to scare her.

Her eyes opened, and she smiled lazily.

"Wow, I must have fallen asleep." She laughed softly, stretching her arms over her head.

"What are you doing out here alone?" Hands in his pockets, he glanced around the barn.

"Being alone," she said simply.

"Ok." He smiled then plopped down next to her. They sat in silence, arms touching. After a time, Faith leaned her head on his shoulder, and he sighed, contented.

"Am I a bad mom?" Her voice sounded strained as she put her hands over her face.

"What? Aw, babe, come here." Pulling her closer, he wrapped his arms around her. "Why would you ever think that?"

"Because I'm hiding out here to be alone, when there's homework to be done, supper to be cooked, laundry to be washed." A single tear slid down her cheek.

"Faith, I know you are a great mom."

"How would you know?" she snorted, wiping the tear away.

"Because I know you and I know that whatever you decide to do, you're great at it. You just can't help yourself. You are determined and strong willed. I've always loved that about you." Jake squeezed her and kissed her head.

"Not everything," he heard her mumble.

"What are you talking about?"

"Marriage. I wasn't so great at that obviously or I wouldn't be sitting here feeling like a total failure as a parent." The misery in her voice had him cursing Gil for being right.

"Last I checked, marriage takes two people. I don't believe for a minute that it didn't work out because of you." Her marriage was the last thing he wanted to discuss but he hated to see her so upset.

"But I left. I couldn't do it anymore, Jake. That's what my kids are going to remember. I left him."

Jake considered, not knowing exactly what to say. He had heard rumors of course, but he wasn't sure what the truth of it was. Having been pushed aside himself, he wondered about the reason.

"Why did you leave, Faith?" His voice sounded hoarse.

"He cheated, more than once. At first, it hurt. Then I got mad. Then one day, I realized I didn't even care anymore. I didn't care. It was awful." She looked up at him, searching for understanding.

He didn't have the nerve to tell her he had been asking about himself. 'Why did you leave me?', his heart screamed, but he didn't think he could take the pain of an honest answer. If she really didn't care about him, he wasn't sure he wanted to know. Swallowing the emotions, he just held her.

"I took them from their dad, and I feel so guilty," she whispered into his chest.

"Faith, you did the right thing for your kids. One day, they'll understand. You brought them home to a family that will love them and help you get through this."

There were so many things he wanted to add. Like how right it felt to hold her. How it should have been him and how she should have never left. But for now, he would be content that she was here in his arms, leaning on him and knowing there was hope for them.

CHAPTER 6

"What's going on with you?" Serena demanded as soon as she opened the door to let Faith in. Her dark ringlets hung loose, framing Serena's heart shaped face and adding to the exotic look of her near black eyes. Faith had met the mysterious Serena through Claire. They had quickly bonded over pizza, a tarot card reading, and plans to get Claire and Evan together.

The house or whatever spirit resided there had brought them closer whenever it revealed to them the houses' name, Coeur du Bayou. Faith still got goosebumps sometimes when she thought of the spooky things that went on here. This house seemed to have a mind of its own, and she was drawn to it.

"Nothing. Why?" Faith gave Serena a guilty look. Serena watched her closely in that patient way that made it seem she already knew everything. She was just waiting for you to say it out loud.

"I've been calling you since yesterday. You never called me back or even sent me a text."

"Oh, I left my phone at home." Faith slid past Serena into the foyer, feeling the house welcome her. She took in the rich dark wood of the sweeping staircase as she explained, "Yesterday was insane. I had a cake to deliver before work and I had a flat. Just another crazy day in my life."

Serena nodded, pursing her lips.

"What?"

"It's ok, Faith. We don't have to talk about it."

"Ugh... about what?"

"Anything." Serena smiled and walked off to the kitchen. "Just know I'm here if you ever want to talk about it."

"I don't know what you mean." Faith followed after Serena, sighing when she entered the kitchen. This kitchen was like a dream. As much as the rest of house creeped her out at times, this kitchen was like a safe haven. Bright and roomy, it made her smile and feel like everything was right with the world. The house may have been named Coeur du Bayou, but this kitchen definitely had her heart. Sighing again, Faith sat at the large island counter while Serena went straight to the coffee pot and poured two cups.

"You might think you're hiding it well, but I pick up on things."

"What are you talking about it?"

"Faith, you've got a lot going on. The divorce, the kids, work, your parents. You can talk to me." Serena handed her a cup, and motioned to the creamer and sugar.

"The divorce will be final soon. I just want it to be over. The kids are adjusting. Work is just work, but I enjoy it. My parents have been wonderful. I just wish Mom would have let us buy her a new oven. My baking has been a nightmare and you know how serious I am about baking." She watched the spoonful of sugar disappear into the black coffee as she stirred.

Serena's musical laugh filled the kitchen, reminding Faith that she wasn't the only one with problems.

"Besides, you have enough problems of your own. The ghost still sabotaging the renovations?"

"Nothing too serious. I know there has to be a reason for it. That room..." she looked up at the ceiling, "I just wish I could put it together. I had thought I'd have it up and running by now, and I guess I could open without that room being finished, but it's just not right."

"I'm sure you and the house will figure it out." Faith smiled at Serena over her coffee cup, then took a sip.

"There, that's better." Letting out a sigh, Serena sat with her coffee.

"What's better?"

"You. You were so tense and stressed when you got here. I could feel it. You're more relaxed now."

"Yeah, I guess so." Shrugging, Faith wondered if she'd ever be able to relax again.

"So, the oven thing. I've been thinking about something and I'd like to talk to you about it."

"Ok?" Faith asked curiously.

"Why don't you bake here in my kitchen?"

"Really?" Faith squeaked at the unexpected question.

"Your mom and her oven are a constant stress. I can see it."

"No, we get along fine," Faith started to argue.

"Yes, but that's her kitchen, her oven. I'm sure she's just like you and doesn't take kindly to someone taking over her territory."

"Oh, wow. I guess I never thought about it like that."

"And this is a commercial kitchen just sitting here. I had it put in up to code because I had hoped to be cooking for the guests. It might be awhile before I get to the guest part." Serena rolled her eyes, then smiling swept a graceful arm out. "Bake here. Set up like you want. I'll give you a key so you can come and go like you need to."

"You really mean it?" Faith looked around in disbelief.

"Yes, I do. That's why I tried to call you yesterday. I've been thinking about it and I know how much you love my kitchen. I think you need to be here and I'm not using it."

"Wow." Faith jumped from her stool and hugged Serena. "This is so great!"

Her black ponytail bobbed up and down as she did a little jig. "So when... I mean I have more baking for the diner and another cake next week. I was dreading using that oven again."

Serena laughed in her easy way and put a key out on the counter. "Whenever you need."

Faith beamed. This was exciting. This gave her hope. Things could definitely be looking up. A big roomy kitchen to work in and spring would be here any day.

"Now, that's settled. I can't help with the divorce. I'll leave that nasty business to the lawyers." Serena picked up her mug again and blew on the hot liquid. Faith picked hers up too, smiling over her cup.

"So, now tell me where you disappear to?"

Faith froze, the hot steam warming her face as she looked up at Serena. Her almond eyes now huge.

"Ah... what... what do you mean?" she stammered.

"You're never around, and no one knows where you are. When we ask you, you give some bullshit answer and change the subject really fast." Placing her cup on the counter, she waited for an answer.

Faith put her mug down slowly, biting her lip. "It's really no big deal."

"Is it a guy? The one from the card readings?"

"No." Serena had read her Tarot cards a few times. Each time they mentioned someone from her past. Jake. She shook her head not wanting to replay the memories again. "It's nothing like that. I have a spot I go to when I need to think. That's all."

Serena narrowed her dark eyes at Faith, "Are you sure?"

"Yes. I'm sure."

"Hello? You guys here?" Claire called from the foyer.

"Back here!" Serena answered never taking her eyes off of Faith. Not being able to meet her gaze, Faith stared into her coffee.

A glowing, happy Claire ran into the kitchen gasping for breath, her cheeks flushed from the cold outside. Her ivory skin made her blue eyes even more brilliant. Her full lips completed the picture reminding Faith of a fairy tale princess. Her brother was a lucky man. Slow, but lucky.

"Guess what?" Not waiting for them to guess, Claire blurted out, "We're pregnant!"

Stunned, the friends sat mouths hanging open and silent. Serena moved first, getting up to hug her friend. "Oh, hun. That's awesome. I just didn't think you guys were trying just yet."

"No, it was a total accident but I'm so excited." Claire shook her head, her dark brown hair falling over her eyes.

Breathe. Breathe. Faith chanted trying to make herself move as she sucked in air through her nose. "Does that mean he finally asked you to marry him?" she choked out the words.

Claire's face changed immediately, going into full pout. "No, why..."

"I don't know if Momma dropped him on his head or what. He is so slow. I'm going talk to him right now. When Mom hears about this, it's not gonna..." Ranting, Faith headed for the door.

"Oh my God! No, Faith." Claire shouted, holding out her hands in front of her. "I'm not pregnant. Rosie is. We left her in the kennel with Red. We didn't know she was in heat."

The glare Faith sent Claire would have finished melting the ice off the trees outside.

Serena doubled over with laughter, as she reached for Faith before she could walk away.

"Your face was priceless. Both of you."

"That was so not funny," Faith said without emotion and walked out of the room.

Stomping into the foyer, she puffed out an angry breath. Surprised when she could see it forming before her. She didn't remember it being so cold in here. Rubbing her arms, she stopped and looked around. Did Claire leave the door open? Ditzy as she was, maybe so. Faith snorted to herself. Turning toward the mirror, she froze, a silent scream in her throat.

The form of a woman stared back at her. The woman was behind her looking over her shoulder into the mirror. *Breathe. Breathe.* Faith spun quickly, the hairs on her neck standing straight up. No one was there. A door slammed upstairs followed by the sounds of weeping.

Faith stood, feet glued to the floor, mouth gaping. Serena and Claire came rushing into the foyer, stopping short at the sounds from above.

"Faith, are you ok?"

"I don't know," Faith whispered still unable to move from the shock.

"What happened?" Claire peered from behind Serena looking around curiously.

"Do you hear that?" Faith asked, needing confirmation that she wasn't crazy.

"Yes." Claire nodded. The weeping faded and the room turned warm.

"Did y'all feel that?" Rubbing at the goosebumps on her arms, Faith shivered.

"Faith, come back to the kitchen and sit. You look like you've seen a ghost." Serena's voice was calm and reassuring, but her eyes were on the second floor landing.

Faith turned back to the mirror frantically looking for a sign of the woman she had seen. "I did."

"Did what, hun?" Serena asked softly.

"I saw a ghost."

CHAPTER 7

"Sis, you ok?"

Faith woke to her brother leaning over her holding a wet towel to her head. His dark bangs fell over his forehead as he watched her. The concern in his face scared her.

"Evan..." she tried to focus, but his broad shoulders blocked everything else out. "What's going on? The kids?"

"They're fine. They're with Mom. You fainted." His voice was unusually patient as he explained.

"What?" Faith sat up straight finally recognizing where she was. Serena's parlor. Feeling dizzy she put a hand to her head. "I don't understand."

"Maybe we should take her to the ER." Evan grimaced over his shoulder at Claire.

"No, I'm fine. Just give me a minute." Faith squeezed her eyes shut to stop the room from spinning.

"Tell me the last thing you remember," Evan said gently.

"I was leaving and I saw...." Her dark eyes grew huge as she looked up at her brother. She grabbed his arm and squeezed. "I saw a ghost. There was a woman in the mirror. She was standing behind me."

Faith heard gasps from Serena and Claire. Her brother frowned down at her in disbelief.

"Are you sure she didn't hit her head?" Evan looked to Serena for an explanation.

"No, but I'm pretty sure Mom dropped you on yours," Faith snorted.

"You're not making any sense. Do you know where you are?" His gruff tone returned.

"Of course," she snapped. "In the parlor... with a candlestick. Oh wow. How cool is that? Serena hit Richie in the head in the parlor with a candlestick." She giggled to herself. Everyone went out of their way to never mention Richie or what happened here, but suddenly the reference to the board game Clue struck her funny.

"You're not making any sense," Evan repeated himself.

"And you're slow, Brother Dear." She grinned at him. "Don't you have something to ask Claire?"

"Shut up, Faith." Glaring, he stood throwing the towel into her lap. "She's fine. Let's go, Darlin'."

"No, I don't think she should be driving." Claire was watching her closely. "Right Serena?"

"Hmmm?" Serena had been sitting quietly staring off into space.

"Maybe she shouldn't drive," Claire said again.

Ignoring Claire's worries, Evan turned back to Faith. "Dad told me you had a flat yesterday. I was looking for you to make sure you took care of it. He was worried that you were still driving on that spare."

"I did. First thing this morning."

"He was worried because you never went back home." His aggravation with his sister was obvious, his voice becoming louder and more suspicious.

"I had to come see Serena. We had business to discuss." Faith held the cool towel to her head again.

"Business? What business?" Claire pouted. "Without me?"

"Faith," Serena interrupted, "Are you sure you're ok?"

"Yes, I'm fine."

"You'll have to tell me what the woman looked like," Serena said absently then waved her hand. "I have some questions, but we can talk later."

"I want to know, too. Why all the secrets?" Claire looked from one friend to the other.

"No, secrets here," Faith said holding up her hands. "Serena offered for me to do my baking here. So that will make Mom happy. As soon as the divorce is final and everything is settled, I'll look for my own place. That'll really make her happy."

"Mom doesn't want to you to leave. She loves having you and the kids there," Evan interjected.

"No, I think you like me being there, so Mom doesn't fuss over you." She swung the towel in his direction.

"You're going to bake here, like a business? Y'all are going into business together?" Claire asked.

"No...well, I don't think it's a business." Faith looked at Serena in awe. "Wow." She felt a spark of hope burst forth.

"Something else to talk about." Serena smiled at her.

"But not without me," Claire insisted.

"I thought we were going to your mom's?" Evan reminded her, then shrugged indifferently. "But that's ok with me if you want to change plans."

"No, we have got to go. Mom's waiting on us." Claire looked from Faith to Serena frowning.

"Dinner with the in-laws?" Faith teased, raising her eyebrows at Evan.

"Cut it out."

"Ok let's go, Evan, but I want to know everything when we get back," Claire insisted again.

"Yeah, you two love birds go ahead. If anything else happens, I'll call Dad."

"About that, Dad doesn't need to be changing your flats," Evan called over his shoulder as he walked from the room.

"He didn't," Faith snapped.

Surprised Evan turned back to his sister. "You changed it?"

"Don't look at me like that." Faith narrowed her eyes at her brother. "I am capable of changing my own tire. How did Dad even know about it?"

"Have you forgotten what's it's like to live in Cypress Point? It was probably all over town before you got it changed. Let's go, Darlin'." Evan guided Claire to the door.

"Safe trip you guys!" Serena called after them.

"Thanks. We'll be back tomorrow afternoon," Claire said as she looked back at them wistfully.

Serena and Faith watched them leave. As soon as the heavy door shut, Serena turned to Faith. "You'd better start talking."

"The ghost?"

"Who changed your tire and is that what this is about?" Pointing a slender finger at Faith, Serena's eyes glittered.

"Who cares who changed my tire? What does that matter?" Picking up the towel again she dapped it to her forehead.

"Faith, I could tell by the guilty look on your face, you did not change that tire. So who did? And why don't you want anyone to know?"

"Ugh. Ok, Ok. I was delivering the cake and I had a flat. Jake happened by and he helped me. No big deal."

"Jake? If it's no big deal why didn't you say that to Evan?" Serena looked back at the door.

"Evan and Jake don't get along. Ancient history stuff. Not worth getting him upset over it."

"And your dad?"

"What about him?" Not following Serena's questions, Faith wondered if she had hit her head.

"Why didn't you tell him?"

"I didn't have my phone to call anyone and it was late by the time I got home." She shrugged as she thought out loud, "I don't know how he even knew about it."

"Ok." Serena shook her head slowly. "I don't think that's everything, but you'll tell me when you're ready. I guess that leaves the ghost. Tell me what happened."

Faith stood on shaky legs and began to pace, trying to recall.

"I left the kitchen and when I got to the foyer, it was freezing. I looked around thinking the door was open. When I looked in the mirror there was a woman standing behind me. Looking at me, watching me."

Rubbing her arms, Faith shivered. "I turned around and she was gone. Then the door upstairs slammed and the crying started. You guys were there for that, right?"

Serena nodded, "Tell me what she looked like."

"Dark hair, it was pulled back, but not a ponytail. It was like..... I don't know. Maybe a bun. Her eyes were dark. Sharp. Piercing. It's like she wanted something from me. You live here. Have you seen her?"

"No, actually I haven't. I know she's here. I've felt her presence but she's never shown herself to me. I don't think you realize how rare this is."

Faith gulped. "Really?"

"Yes, and I've noticed something else. The only time she cries is when you are here."

"No, you heard her." Faith sat back on the couch pulling her legs up under her. "So did Claire."

"But only when you are here. The doors slam for me, yes. The crying only started when you came here." Serena got up and pulled a book from the shelf. "Remember you were the first to hear it. Now you've seen her."

"You're freaking me out, Serena." Hugging her knees to her chest, she closed her eyes again.

"I'm just trying to figure out why." Serena sat with the notebook on her lap lost in her thoughts.

"I don't know."

They sat in silence thinking it over. The only sounds Faith could hear were the house settling and the faint singing of birds from outside. The house seemed to be at peace for the moment.

"You write it down?" Faith asked curiously.

"Hmm.. Oh yeah," Serena answered noticing the book in her hands. "I keep a journal of when things happen. Record the date and time. To see if there's a certain time where there's more activity."

The way Serena said the word activity so casually, chilled Faith to her core. "Oh. So it's not all the time?"

"No. Why?" Serena opened the book and began to flip through the pages. Her face crestfallen she asked, "Are you having second thoughts about using my kitchen?"

"Actually no," Faith declared surprised at her own answer.

"Really? You were pretty freaked out."

"Yeah, at first, but I love that kitchen. I think I need this. Some space you know? For the first time since my separation I feel like there is hope for the future. My future."

Serena smiled sadly. "I know what you mean. This house has been that for me. I'm glad to share that with you. Ghost and all. Let me get your key." Standing she added, "If you ever need to come and stay, bring the kids. Just let me know."

"Don't say that in front of my kids. They'll be packing their bags." Faith laughed as Serena exited the room.

In the months that had followed Serena's first offer of a sleepover, her kids had bugged her relentlessly to sleep in the haunted house. Trent had bullied Evan into agreeing to camp out in the woods, but Evan had successfully put him off so far. She groaned again thinking of her brother and how he was dragging his feet with the marriage proposal, too. She knew she shouldn't push, but he needed a shove. She grinned.

Returning with the key, Serena noticed her smile. "What's that look for? What are you plotting?"

"My brother owes Trent a campout. I'm going to make sure he gets it, if you don't mind."

"Not at all. Here's your key." Holding out her hand, the key sat upon Serena's palm. The air suddenly became heavy around them as if the house itself was holding its breath.

Faith breathed in and reached for it. This key held more meaning to her than just an open door. It held the magic of hope.

As her hand touched the metal, Serena wrapped her hands around Faith's. "It's going to be ok. I know it," she whispered forcefully as if hearing her thoughts. Her dark eyes bored into Faith's. Stunned at the sudden intensity of Serena's actions, Faith drew another sharp breath. This time she caught the faint smell of gardenias.

CHAPTER 8

"Really Mom? You mean it?" Trent jumped up and down on the worn linoleum floor of her mother's kitchen.

"Of course. Miss Serena said it was ok and your birthday is coming up. I think we should have it before it gets too hot."

"What about Uncle Evan? Did you ask him?" Trent bit his lip nervously.

"He said he'd do it. We'll just remind him when he gets here."

"When's he coming?" Trent asked looking out of the kitchen window, willing his uncle to appear. There was no way Evan would be able to talk his way out of it now.

Gazing at her son, Faith marveled at the perfect mix of David and herself. Not just their looks, but characteristics as well. Both determined and, what had Jake called her, strong willed. At one time, maybe. Having children had changed her and left her so overwhelmed. Most days she felt one step away from a nervous breakdown.

Her heart warmed and filled with pride as she watched her son. There were mannerisms and facial expressions that were totally David. She thought back to when they first met, both young and vibrant college students with dreams of a wonderful life ahead. Her plans changed as soon as they were engaged. The wedding, which turned into a huge affair, took almost full time planning. Deciding to take a semester off, until after the wedding, the time flew by. After the wedding she was Mrs. David Williams, and she was happy. Supporting her husband and his dreams became her dream. When she discovered she was pregnant, she felt her life was complete. David had been so excited at becoming a father, her hopes for the life she planned became reality. He was an excellent father. He worked hard to support them and they wanted for nothing. Two years later, their happiness grew when Hannah was born. They were the perfect family.

Faith had spent hours upon hours trying to figure out when and how things started to change. A whiff of perfume on his clothes when sorting laundry, she'd chalk it up to her imagination. The late night meetings became more frequent along with out of town trips. She confronted him. He denied it. Things would go back to normal for a while, then the mysterious phone calls and emergency meetings would start up again. She'd confront. He'd deny. He went as far as implying she was crazy and hormonal. She had kept up appearances and held her tongue. Somewhere in those years she had lost herself. She'd look in the mirror and wonder what became of the girl that wasn't afraid of anything and certainly not afraid to speak her mind. As the kids grew, she took classes to pass the time. Painting, pottery, and cake decorating. She loved to make things with her hands. It kept her mind occupied and not focused on the fact that her life had become a lie. She hadn't meant for it to be this way. This was not the life she had imagined for herself. She was married to a stranger, that had a separate life from the one she was living. She cooked for him, did his laundry and took care of his children, but she felt as if she never really knew him. Once the hurt wore off, she became angry, distant and uncaring.

The day she found the red lacy underwear in his pocket she didn't feel a thing. Not even surprise. She washed them with his clothes, folded them and tucked them into his dresser drawer without so much as a gasp, curse word, or a single tear. That's when she knew it was time for her to leave. Time to take her life back.

"I'm going to tell Paw Paw." Trent had been talking nonstop about his plans for the campout.

"Sure. I'm sure he'd love to hear about it. Let's go find him." Getting up from the table, she peeked into the living room where Hannah was sitting mesmerized by the latest Disney movie. Faith followed Trent out to the backyard. She knew they would find her father tinkering in his shop. Half way there, they heard Evan's truck in the driveway. Trent turned around making a beeline for his uncle. Nearing the shop, Faith called out to her father, "Dad?"

"Yeah." Only his eyes moved to greet her. His strong capable hands held together a rocking chair with a missing leg. "You get that tire fixed?"

"Yes, sir. I saw about that yesterday." She wasn't surprised the tire was the first thing he asked about. Ed Bertrand was not known for leaving things undone or broken.

"Good." His concentration immediately returned to the task in front of him, he eyed the replacement leg.

"How did you know about that?"

"Jake came by to let us know. Said he didn't want us to worry in case we tried to reach you. You didn't have your phone." He frowned at Faith then chiseled another sliver of wood off the leg.

"Oh. He came here?" Faith didn't bother to hide her surprise.

"Yeah. He said he was going to put the spare on for you, so I didn't worry."

"Oh."

"Everything ok, Sister?" Her father looked up from the workbench curiously.

"Yeah, I just didn't know he had come by." Faith glanced at the doorway of the shop. "Was Evan here?"

"No."

She could hear Trent's excited voice and Evan's laughter from across the yard, getting closer. "Ok. Ok. I'll have to check my work schedule but I promise we'll do it, if that's what you want."

"Yeah!" Trent's triumphant shout sounded as he appeared in the doorway. "Paw Paw, guess what?"

"What?" This time Ed looked up with a smile for his grandson.

"I'm going to have a campout for my birthday and sleep in a tent and have a fire, right Uncle Evan?" Getting it all out in one breath, Trent smiled up at his uncle.

"Sure, it'll be a guy's only thing. No girls allowed." Evan gave Trent a playful shove.,

"Fine by me," Faith said rolling her eyes. "I'll make the cake. We can do that in the house or on the porch."

"Here?" Her father looked up worried.

"No, not here. At Serena's."

"Oh." Having the answer he wanted, Ed turned back to the project before him. "Where's your mom?"

"I'm sure she's checking on dinner. She was inside somewhere. Hannah's watching TV." Faith watched as he fit the leg into the seat of the rocker and pulled it out again.

"I'm going to tell her about my campout," Trent exclaimed running off to find his grandmother.

"So, how was the trip?" Faith asked casually, ready to harass her brother.

"It was nice. Made good time coming home." Evan leaned over to watch Ed's work.

"That's a nice drive. Probably a lot has changed since I've been that way," her father commented sanding the rough edges.

"Probably so," Evan agreed and handed the wood glue to his father.

"And the visit?" she prompted.

"Great. Claire and her mom got to see each other. That's all that matters."

Faith smiled at her brother. She couldn't even tease him. Standing there over their father, the resemblance was uncanny. Not just in their features, but their attitudes. They both had a caring, helpful and protective nature. Evan would make a wonderful father. He had a great role model. She wondered about Trent, what kind of man would he grow to be. She desperately hoped that some of that honest caring nature would rub off on him. Maybe Jake was right. Ugh. Jake. *'Let's not go there,'* she said to herself.

"I'm glad y'all had a good trip. I'll go find Mom before I go to work." She blinked away the tears that had started to form.

"Tell her I'll be there in a minute. I'm almost done here."

"Ok, Dad." Faith kissed him on the cheek. "See ya' later. Bye Evan."

"Hey, you remember your phone this time," her dad called after her.

"Yes, sir."

Faith laughed to herself as she thought that some things would never change. She would probably still be reminding her kids even when they were grown, too. They would always be her kids. The thought warmed her as she opened the back door.

"Faith Ann." Oh boy. Mom sounded upset. Not mad exactly, but sorely disappointed.

"Yes?" Faith took a deep breath while still standing in the laundry room, before stepping into the kitchen.

"What's this about going into business with Serena? You said you were just going to bake over there, so I'd have my kitchen for Sunday dinner. You didn't say anything."

"Mom...." Faith sighing, glanced over at Claire who was sitting red faced at the kitchen table.

"I'm sorry," Claire mouthed.

"And then Trent comes in here telling me about a camp out for his party. No girls? Hannah's upset."

"Geesh, Mom. Don't you want your kitchen back? Serena just offered for me to use her kitchen to bake my cakes and stuff for the diner. I'd have more room and I won't be making a mess in your kitchen. I don't know anything about a business. We haven't even talked about it." She glared at Claire.

"And as far as the party, Evan promised him and he's the one that said no girls," she added throwing him into the mix. "Besides, Trent is getting older. It should be for him and his friends. Guy things."

"But he'll have a cake?"

"Of course." Faith rolled her eyes. "You know, you never let me tag along with Evan and his friends."

The door slammed as Evan strode into the room.

"And there was a good reason for that, Sis." Evan's dark eyes fixed on her.

Oh great. Here it comes. Her dad, man of few words as he was, had obviously let slip who changed the tire.

"You didn't tell me it was Jake that changed your tire." His angry tone made Claire gasp.

"Is that a question?" Faith asked flippantly.

"No, Dad just told me." He towered over her with his hands on his hips.

"So what's the big deal? He helped me out."

"Faith don't start that up again. You know what the big deal is. You didn't listen to me then and look how that turned out." Evan's voice was low but mincing.

"And it's still none of your business, Brother Dear. I've got to go to work." Turning to her mother. "I have my phone, tell Dad. Call if y'all need me."

Her mother smiled uncomfortably. "Ok, Dear. Don't worry. They're fine."

Without looking back she left the room to find her kids. She kissed them both, after making sure their things were ready for the next morning. Grabbing her jacket, and double checking to make sure she had her phone, she walked back through the kitchen.

Evan and Claire sat at the kitchen table, her mother was at the stove. Evan still fuming watched her enter the room. Margaret had probably fussed at him. Claire's big blue eyes watched miserably. Faith couldn't help herself as she reached the laundry room doorway. She blurted out casually, "Oh, yeah, since we're sharing news, did they tell you, Mom? You're gonna be a grandma again."

The horrified look on Evan's face and Claire's opened mouthed silent gasp had her giggling as she ran out of the house, her ponytail bobbing all the way to her car.

CHAPTER 9

Jake entered the diner sounding the familiar jingle of the bell on the door. He had circled the diner several times that day hoping to see her again. Unable to keep his mind off of Faith all day, he was relieved to finally see her car in the parking lot.

"Back again?" Faith walked towards him taking the order pad out of her apron pocket.

"Man's gotta eat," Jake said easily sliding into a chair at the counter.

"I'm surprised you can find time to eat with all those status reports you have to file. But I guess making sure my parents are up to date makes for a hungry boy." She slapped the pad down onto the counter.

After their honest talk in the barn yesterday, Jake was taken by surprise at her brisk tone. "Wha... Wait, was that secret? Like the barn?" He added the last part in a whisper.

"No, it wasn't a secret, but I didn't think you'd go to my house and tell my dad." Her head bobbed with attitude making her ponytail dance.

"Think about it. You didn't have your phone. If someone would have seen your car out there and told your dad he would have worried. Next he'd have half the town out looking for you. You know he doesn't like to drive after dark."

"Yeah, you're right. How do you know he doesn't like driving after dark? I didn't realize y'all are like BFF's." Her snappy comeback left Jake wondering who had ruffled her feathers.

"You may have left, Faith, but life didn't stop here. I've never stopped talking to your dad. Even when Evan was being an ass." He regretted his terse reply, but her misplaced anger wasn't sitting well with him. Watching the range of emotions flicker across her face, Jake waited patiently.

"Oh... " Faith shrugged her shoulders.

Jake realized it had probably never occurred to her that he still talked to Ed. She'd really be surprised to know that he still talked to Evan on occasion.

"What do y'all talk about?" The curious expression on Faith's face made him chuckle out loud.

"Well, let me think... hmmm." He pretended to recall while watching her aggravation grow. "You know what, that's not really your business, nosey. How about taking my order?"

"Let me guess, the usual?" The fiery glare she sent him erupted a sudden rush of desire.

"Sounds great." One of his favorite games had been riling Faith up just to watch her work off the anger, then make her happy again.

The bell over the diner door jingled breaking their staring contest but the heat building between them lingered.

"Jake, honey, where have you been?" Tracey McMillian's sickly sweet voice zeroed in on Jake.

"Working. Getting the fields ready for planting." Barely glancing in her direction, his gaze was drawn back to Faith.

"I haven't seen you at the bar in ages." Not wanting to be ignored, Tracey leaned on the counter suggestively.

"No, I've been too tired from work." Jake shook his head and grimaced. "I'm not getting any younger."

"Aw, don't go getting all boring on me." She glanced over at Faith then gave Jake a fake pout. "I miss my drinking buddy."

"No chance of that." Jake laughed sitting back in his chair.

"Hey, I heard Amy LeBlue is playing here this weekend. You sitting in?"

"Yeah, thinking about it."

"Ok, good." Turning back to Faith she asked, "Got my order, honey?"

"Yep. Here it is. $16.45" Faith placed the food containers on the counter with a thud and smiled at Tracey. Keeping a smile plastered on her face as the money changed hands.

Tracey smiling back in Jake's direction pushed out her cleavage as she grabbed for her food. "See ya', Jake."

"Yeah, see ya'," Jake said without a second glance. He was too busy watching Faith shoot daggers at the blonde's retreating back. He smiled ear to ear.

"What's that goofy look for?" Faith asked turning back to get his drink order.

"You're jealous."

"Of that?" She pointed at the door, "I don't think so."

"Then why the attitude?" Leaning forward on the counter Jake watched the fireworks in her eyes.

"I don't like her. I never have."

"Because she wants me?"

"Hahahaha. No, because women like that have to push their cleavage out to get noticed."

"Ok, if that's your story."

"Yes, it is. What do you want to drink?" All business now she picked her order pad back up.

"Sweet tea. What are you doing Friday night?"

"Why?" Faith's head snapped up obviously caught off guard by his question.

"Just wondering." He saw the fear in her eyes, and decided against asking her out right on a date. "I sit in with some of the bands. There's a good one playing out here this weekend. You should come check it out."

"I'm working and the kids...." Looking around frantically, she shrugged. "I don't go out."

"Ok, if you change your mind, you should come by."

The door jingled again. A pretty woman with the biggest blue eyes Jake had ever seen entered the diner. Her face was troubled as she approached Faith.

"Hey, what's wrong?" Faith asked immediately concerned.

"Nothing. I just had to come. I'm so sorry. Please don't be mad at me. I should have never opened my mouth," she said her blue eyes glistening with the promise of tears. Jake watched with interest eager to find out who she was.

"Claire." Faith sighed rolling her eyes, "I'm not mad... anymore. Please sit down."

"Are you sure?"

"Yes, I'm sure. I know you ate at Mom's, but you want something to drink? How about some pie on me?" Faith smiled at Claire to reassure her.

"No, I'm good. I can't stand the thought of you being mad at me."

"I'm not, really. It was just a lot at once." Grimacing, she asked, "Evan still pissed?"

"Well...." Claire looked away.

"I know he is. You don't have to say it. I'm sure Mom freaked."

"I didn't know what to do or say. Your mom was hugging me, and Evan was hollering.

Then your dad came in to see what all the noise was about."

"I'm sorry. I couldn't help it. Evan gets all holier than thou and I just lose my shit."

Jake chuckled reminding Faith they had an audience. Obviously this was the infamous Claire that everyone had been searching for on Halloween. Jake had only gotten a glimpse of her as Evan carried her back to the big house that night.

"Yeah, you seem to know how to push his buttons, too." Claire added.

"Well now, this sounds like a great story," Jake interrupted wanting to hear the details.

"Be quiet, Jake." Faith waved a hand at him to shoo him off.

"Jake?" Claire glanced at him curiously.

"Yes, ma'am, at your service. Do tell." He gave Claire a grin then sent a pointed look in Faith's direction. "I like a good story while I wait, since it seems the service is a bit slow tonight."

"Ugh, sorry." Faith hurried off to the kitchen.

"So, you're Jake?" Claire smiled at him shyly.

"The one and only. Has Faith been talking about me?"

"No, but that's what started this whole thing. Faith didn't tell Evan about you changing the tire and he got so mad. Then Faith said we were having a baby and everything just went crazy." She put her hands through her hair and sighed.

"Congratulations, I guess." Jake tried to process the information she had just blurted out.

"No, my dog is having the baby. I mean puppies." She looked around, then asked in a whisper, "Why doesn't Evan..."

"Long story. Maybe you should ask Faith. She's got her secrets." Jake watched Faith moving around in the kitchen through the order window.

"No joke. Not talking seems to be a family trait," Claire agreed.

"So you and Evan. That's great. I wish y'all the best."

"Thanks." Claire smiled widely her eyes shining with happiness. "You and Faith are..."

"..are friends," Jake finished for her. He watched Faith come back through the swinging doors. "Because that's what she needs right now." Turning back to Claire with his lopsided grin he asked, "You like music?"

"Yeah, sure."

"There's a great band playing Friday night. Yours truly is sitting in."

"Really? What do you play?"

"Guitar. Sing a bit, too. You and Evan should come out."

"Oh, I don't know. I'll see," Claire said uncertainly as Faith placed Jake's tea in front of him.

"Evan and I go way back. It's all good." He watched for Faith's reaction as he answered. As she turned away he thought he caught an eye roll.

"Then why did he get so mad?" Claire wondered out loud.

"I'm not good enough for his little sister."

Faith was making her way back to the kitchen when she heard Jake's comment. "What? Why would you think that? Did he say that? Evan doesn't get to say..." She was still grumbling when she went back through the swinging doors.

He grinned and winked at Claire. "See. I think she only dated me to piss him off."

"Oh, I see. You're him." Claire smiled knowingly.

"Him?" Still amused Jake took a sip of his drink.

"Yeah, the love she's going to be reunited with from her past."

Jake nearly spit out his drink.

"Serena's been telling her, but she acts like it's nothing. Just like when she saw the ghost. She tried to act like nothing was wrong. If she's going to be baking there she can't..." Claire stopped in mid-sentence. "Oh, I'm doing it again. Sorry."

"What?" Jake felt dizzy trying to follow her ramblings.

"I should just go before I make her mad again." Claire got up to leave.

"Wait. Where are you going?" Faith called as she came back to the counter, carrying Jake's order.

"I should go. I shouldn't bother you at work."

"No, sit. Here have some pie." Grabbing Jake's piece of pie, Faith offered it to Claire.

"No. I should go."

"Ok, next time the pie will be on me."

"Can I have my pie back?" Jake asked offended.

"See you Claire." Faith put the pie back in front him and headed back to the kitchen. That was a definite eye roll.

"Nice to meet you, Jake."

"Same here. Tell Evan I said to take you out and stop being such a stick in the mud."

"Well, maybe you should take Faith out. I think she likes to dance, too." She smiled at Jake, her blue eyes twinkling.

"I tried. I'm hoping she'll show up."

"Maybe I can help with that," Claire said as Faith came back out the swinging doors.

"Help with what?"

"Evan," Claire and Jake said at the same time.

"Hmm." Faith snorted, "There's no hope for him."

CHAPTER 10

"Mom, Mom...."

Faith reluctantly drifted into consciousness, the insistent voice and impatient hands of her son pulling at the throw that covered her.

"Mom."

"What is it Trent?" she asked without opening her eyes, wanting to snuggle deeper into the worn couch in her parents living room.

"Dad's on the phone. He needs to talk to you."

"Ok." Sighing sleepily she took the phone from her son and answered, "Hello?"

"Were you sleeping?" Hearing the amusement in her ex-husband's voice she groaned inwardly.

"Oh, yeah, I must have drifted off. What's wrong?"

"Nothing. I thought maybe I'd take the kids this weekend if you don't have anything planned."

His sudden request jolted her awake.

"Well..." She looked up at Trent who was still standing over her and noticed Hannah watching her from behind him, both sets of eyes bright with excitement.

As much as she missed them when they visited their dad, she knew they missed their father and he must miss them terribly.

"Ok, that's fine. What time will you be here to get them?"

"I thought maybe we could meet half way and all have dinner together."

"I don't know. I think I'm scheduled to work and I have a cake."

"We love cake, bring it." His voice distracted, she knew he probably wasn't even listening to what she said.

"No, I have a cake to make for someone."

"Oh. Well, is a few hours going to make that much of a difference? Have the kids pick a place and let me know. Gotta run. See you Friday."

She heard the click of the line disconnecting before she could answer. Typical David. Only hearing what he wanted to hear, and not easily dissuaded.

"We can go, right?" Hannah asked hopefully.

"Of course, I just don't know if I'll be able to bring y'all to meet him. I have to..."

The disappointment on their faces stopped her train of thought. They were just kids. All they knew was the family they had been before. They didn't understand the complications of divorce or the uncomfortable feeling of having to sit through a meal with someone that had betrayed you. She had tried hard to not show any negativity towards their father or bitter feelings on her part, but avoiding him had been the key to her sanity.

At her silence, she saw the hope return to their eyes. She knew she'd change her schedule, and be up all night working on the cake, if that's what it took.

"Ok. Dad said y'all can pick the restaurant."

Shouting with joy and a few victorious fist pumps into the air, they ran from the room.

"What's going on?" Margaret called from the kitchen.

Stretching as she got up from the couch, Faith wandered into the kitchen to meet her mother. "It was David. He wants the kids this weekend."

"Oh.' Her mother turned back towards the stove.

"What?"

"Nothing." Margaret lifted a lid and began to stir.

"I know that 'oh'. Just say it, Mom."

"I was just thinking it wasn't supposed to be this weekend, but I think it's great he wants to see them." Closing the lid again she turned to look at Faith.

"And?"

"And you could use some rest, Faith. You're running yourself ragged, between the diner and the baking."

"Mom, I'm fine." Pulling out a chair, she sat at the table.

"I'm just saying you could use some rest. That's all."

"I just had a great nap. What time is it anyway?" Yawning she looked towards the clock.

"It's almost six. Are you going to your belly dancing class?"

"Ugh.. no I don't think so. I probably should go to Serena's and see what I can do ahead of time, so I can bring the kids on Friday." She had already started making a list of what needed to be done in her head.

"You know, you can use my kitchen," Margaret reminded her.

"Yes, Mom. I appreciate it, but you're making dinner. I'll be in your way. There's way more room over there and I'm thinking if I can take more orders for cakes and stuff, I won't have to work at the diner."

"That would be great. You'll have more time to rest."

"Yeah, that, too." Faith rolled her eyes then asked, "Have you talked to Evan?"

"No, not since Sunday. He's probably still upset with you. You shouldn't have done that."

"I'm sorry Mom. He just doesn't know when to quit. And I don't know why he hasn't popped the question yet. He's so slow."

Margaret shook her head in agreement. "He's always had to do things in his own time. Never liked to be pushed."

"Really?" Faith smiled thinking of Evan as a boy. She had never noticed that trait until recently.

"Oh, yes. You on the other hand, always running head first into whatever you had your mind set on."

Nodding her head in agreement, she knew she couldn't argue with that description. "And Elle?"

Margaret sighed heavily. "Oh, Elle.... she always had to be different, no matter what the cost."

Faith smiled as she thought of her younger sister. Being nine years apart had left a gap more than in just age. She supposed it was because she'd always tried to mother her. They were both grownups now, but still not as close as she would have liked them to be. As soon as she was able, Elle had taken off to parts unknown. Margaret usually had some idea of where she was. Through the years they had never seemed to be in the same place at the same time. Whenever they did manage it, it was uncomfortable at best.

"Where is Elle now?"

"Oh, in Dallas. Still at that radio job. She seems to like it."

"That's good. Is she going to make it for Easter?"

"I hope so. It would be nice to have everyone together for once." Margaret smiled, her face beaming.

Faith was struck with a bout of sadness. One day that would be her. Actually it was her already. Having to alternate the holidays with David had been difficult and downright depressing. Knowing that's what she had to look forward to in the future, filled her with anxiety. Eventually, she'd be alone, when the kids had their own families. Her chest tightened at the thought. *Breathe. Breathe.*

"I got to go." She stood up feeling the need to move.

"Don't you want to eat first?" her mother asked disappointed.

"No, I'll eat later."

"The kids need to eat. Leave them here with me and I'll make sure they have their baths after supper."

"You sure you don't mind?"

"Of course not. I love having y'all here and being able to see y'all every day."

Once again, she felt the tightness as she thought of not seeing her kids every day. She couldn't imagine ever being able to let them go.

"Thanks," she hugged her mother forcefully, whispering in her ear, "I love you, Mom."

"I love you too. It's all going to work out, you'll see." Margaret patted her on the back.

"I know."

Her mother, besides being a fantastic cook, could always be counted on for encouragement and a healthy dose of hope. Faith wiped at her eyes. "Ok, I'm going to go get everything organized so I can bring them Friday after school."

"Do you have your phone?"

Faith laughed, "Yes, and my jacket is in my car. It was really warm today. Maybe spring is here."

Faith was disappointed when she didn't see Serena's car in the driveway, then remembered belly dancing class. They would be wondering where she was. She would use the quiet time to gather her supplies and see what else she needed. If she could get some of it done ahead of time, she knew she wouldn't be so stressed.

Letting herself in with the key Serena gave her, she swung the heavy door open. Walking into the foyer still took her breath away sometimes. The ghost lady hadn't made another appearance but she still felt better when she got to the kitchen.

She knew that keeping herself busy was the only way to combat the anxiety. Mentally making lists of 'To Do's' and 'To Get's'. Planning out each step of the cake process kept her mind and hands busy and gave her something to look forward to. Pulling out the ingredients and pans she went straight to work, humming to herself. A radio would be nice in here she thought as she measured out a cup of flour, then another still humming a tune she didn't recognize. She must have heard it on her dad's radio in the shop and just didn't remember. The melody kept playing in her head as she hummed along. Her movements sure and her measurements precise, she beat the batter into a smooth mixture.

She was pouring the batter into pans when the crying started.

"No," she said out loud. Sadness flooded through her as the weeping continued. The melody in her head played softly as she trembled, unsure what to do. She had never been alone in the house when this happened.

Trying to be brave, she scraped out the mixing bowl and put it in the sink. Humming to herself loudly, she tried to drown out the sound. It never lasted long. Checking the oven to make sure the temperature was right, she stopped cold. Something wasn't right. The music that had been in her head now seemed to be coming from the parlor. She broke out in a cold sweat, forcing herself to move.

Walking slowly out of the kitchen and through the foyer, she didn't dare look into the mirror. She walked quickly past it and into the parlor. *In the parlor with the candle stick.* She laughed to herself nervously. The humorous thoughts flew from her mind as she took in her surroundings. The furnishings were different. In place of Serena's tastefully decorated room was lavish furniture. The drapes were heavy brocade and pulled tight, leaving the room in shadows with only candles giving off light. A silver tea service sat out on the side board. Head spinning, she reached for the nearest curtain, desperate to look outside. The air hung heavily around her as she pushed the folds of the thick material aside. Peering into the darkness outside, she was puzzled. The porch light had been on. Hadn't it? Startled by the sound of movement outside on the porch, she moved away from the window. What the hell was going on? Looking around the room again she didn't recognize anything but the mantle. Everything else had been changed. Creeping quietly to the front door she meant to check the lock, but the knob began to turn as soon as she reached out to touch it. Yanking her hand back, she backed away from the door. Suddenly terrified, she ran up the stairs. The crying continued, she could hear it more clearly as she moved away from the music. Faith found herself in the front bedroom, closing the door behind her.

As she listened for some indication of what was happening downstairs, she glanced around. Serena hadn't told her she finished this room. It was beautifully decorated with an antique bed and washstand. A wooden rocker was placed in front of the window as if someone had been watching and waiting. Not hearing footsteps, or anyone calling out, she was afraid again. Going to the window to see if she could see a car in the drive, she peered out cautiously. The music had faded, but the crying continued. The dark outside seemed infinite and she trembled at the cold of the glass against her hand. She sat numbly in the rocker, dazed and disoriented. The crying grew louder, and made her so sad. She hugged herself as she rocked, suddenly realizing the crying was coming from her. She was sobbing uncontrollably, muttering the words, "My baby. My baby."

The sadness was overwhelming as she slid out of the chair and to her knees.

"I want my baby."

CHAPTER 11

"Son of a bitch," Jake cursed, the wrench slipping out of his hands again and clattering to the floor of the small pump shed. Buzzing from his coat pocket interrupted his rant. Seeing Faith's name on the screen, cleared all the angry thoughts and put a smile on his face. There was hope. She was calling him.

"Hey, babe."

"J..j..jake."

The pump, wrench and everything was completely wiped from his thoughts.

"What's wrong Faith?" already moving towards his truck, he asked worriedly.

"I don't know..." Her broken sobs wrenched at his heart.

"Tell me where you are. I'm coming."

"I don't know what's happening to me... I'm at Serena's."

"Ok, I'm coming just stay put."

She was still sobbing into the phone when he pressed the end button. Terrified he drove as fast as he could, leaving clouds of dust in the blackness of his rear view mirror. Screeching into the drive of the old house, his door was open before the truck came to a stop. A light came on under the massive porch as he ran up the steps.

"Faith!"

Reaching for the door, it opened before he could grab the handle. It creaked as it swung slowly into the foyer. Not seeing anyone, he stepped inside and called out again.

"Faith?"

His answer was a muffled sobbing that came from somewhere upstairs. He took the sweeping staircase two steps at a time, calling out again at the landing.

"Faith, I'm here."

Her crying led him to the unfinished bedroom where she was huddled on the floor.

"Oh, Jake." Her relief was evident as she jumped up and into his arms. He held her, looking around for any clue to what was going on.

"Faith? Are you hurt?" he asked rubbing her arms.

"No." Her answer was muffled as she spoke into his chest.

"Can you tell me what's wrong?" Jake asked gently pulling her away from him, trying to get answers.

"I don't know. I don't know what's happening to me."

"Tell me."

"I was baking in the kitchen and I heard music. Someone was on the porch and I got scared. I came up here and there was crying... I didn't know it was me. I just..." Her dark eyes searched the room. "This wasn't like this. There was a bed and a rocking chair. I'm not crazy."

Jake shook his head, looking around the room. "You're not crazy." He hugged her close trying to reassure her. "Let's go downstairs and you can explain it again."

"Faith?" A voice called from downstairs.

"We're here," Jake called down, walking Faith out of the room to the landing.

"Oh." Serena watched them curiously as they made their way down the stairs. "What happened?"

"I'm not sure." Jake recognized the owner of the house from their brief meeting on Halloween night. Faith had been upset and crying then too.

"Did you see her again?" Serena asked Faith.

"See who?" Jake's question went unanswered as the friends continued to talk.

"No, but it was so strange," Faith said finally calming down.

"Did you pass out again?" Serena's dark eyes were filled with concerned.

"No, it was like being caught in a dream, and you can't wake up. But I was awake." Faith wiped at her face as she tried to explain.

"Come to the kitchen," Serena offered.

At the mention of the kitchen, Faith drew in a sharp breath. "Oh my God, did I burn the cakes?" She ran past them both to the kitchen, sighing with relief when she saw the batter still sitting in the pans. After putting the pans in the oven, she turned to Jake and Serena. "I hadn't put them in yet. It felt like it had been a long time."

"Maybe you should sit." Serena looked from Faith to Jake. "I can make tea or something."

"Oh, sorry. Serena this is Jake. Jake this is Serena. This is her house." Faith made the introductions.

"Nice to meet you. Faith sure has some pretty friends," Jake said easily, giving her his lopsided grin.

"Um, thanks," Serena said uncomfortably with a hesitant smile.

"I met Claire a few days ago," he added quickly.

"Ah, ok." Serena's smile widened for a brief second then a worried look settled back across her face. "Faith you still look pale. Maybe you should sit."

"No, just let me pick up this mess while the cake is in the oven. I'm glad I didn't burn it. I would have had to start over." Faith moved around the kitchen nervously picking up dirty bowls and utensils. Glancing at the clock, she asked in surprise, "Oh, is belly dancing over already?"

"Yes. Maybe for good, but I don't want to talk about that right now," Serena said waving her hand to dispel the thought.

"What happened? They can't cancel the class."

"No, not cancel, but replace. Ever heard of Zumba!? I'd have to get certified, and I'm not interested in doing that right now." She waved her hand again, "Enough about that. I want to hear what happened."

"Yeah, maybe you can explain to me," Jake said sliding onto a stool at the island.

Faith started with hearing the music, and walked through what happened.

Jake sat quietly listening in amazement. Serena had jumped up to get a notebook from another room and was scribbling furiously as Faith continued with her story.

"Ok, so the parlor was different?"

"Yeah, and the upstairs bedroom. I thought you had finished it and never told me. It was beautiful." Faith stared off into space as a wistful smile crossed her face.

"Really? You can describe it to me later. You said someone was on the porch?"

"Yeah I looked out the window and I could hear someone out there. It scared me for some reason. I went to make sure the door was locked but someone turned the knob."

"You?" Serena pointed to Jake with her pen.

"No, when I got here she was upstairs."

"No, it wasn't him. I called him after. I don't know who. I never saw anyone, but I was terrified. I ran to that room."

"And it was different?"

"Yes, I loved it. There was this beautiful rocker by the window."

"Faith, you were crying when you called me. I could barely understand you." Jake was perplexed at her sudden cheery mood.

"Crying?" Serena's head snapped up from the notebook. "Crying in that room?"

"Yes, I heard the crying like before. Then it was me crying. I couldn't stop. I was so sad." The color drained from her face remembering. "I was crying for my baby. I wanted my baby." Faith clutched at her stomach obviously relieving the pain she had felt.

"Oh, Faith." Serena got up and went to her, "You were crying. You didn't see her because you *were* her."

"What? No, I was me," Faith said pointing to her chest.

"Of course, but what you were seeing wasn't now. It had to be then." Serena's dark eyes glittered with excitement. "Don't you see? She's trying to show you why she cries."

"Her baby," Faith whispered.

"Yes, but why you? Hmmm. You're a mother too. Maybe." She went back to her notebook and scribbled some more. Looking up at Jake she asked, "She called you?"

"Yeah."

"And you were the one that brought her back to the house Halloween night?"

"Yeah." He shifted nervously under Serena's gaze. Damn. That must be what a fly under a microscope feels like. He liked it better when they were ignoring him. "Why?"

"Oh, I just recognized you. I thought you looked familiar," she answered shrugging her shoulders.

Somehow, Jake knew that was not all she was thinking. She knew something, but what, he didn't know. He knew women looked at him, and he never minded. This was different. This unnerved him.

"Faith, I gotta go," Jake said suddenly standing. "Are you ok?"

"Yeah, I'm fine. I'm sorry I made you come running like that. I didn't know who else to call."

Serena made a small noise. When Jake turned toward her, she was smiling.

"It was so nice to meet you, Jake. I hope I'll see you again soon." Her statement seemed genuine. Wondering at the change in her, he smiled back.

"Belly dancing? So you like to dance?" he asked.

It was her turn to look uncomfortable. "Yes, I do," she answered him slowly.

"Faith, bring her with you on Friday night. It'll be fun."

"Friday?" Serena asked looking at Faith.

"Yeah, I'm sitting in with a band down at the bar. You should come," Jake suggested.

"Jake, I told you I can't make it," Faith said confused.

"Gil told me you asked for Friday off." He smiled at her slyly.

"Oh. Not for that. I have to bring my kids to meet David. We're having dinner."

He winced at the pain before he could stop himself. Forcing himself to stand straight and look at her, he answered, "I didn't know."

A door slammed above them, making them all jump.

"No," Faith squeaked grabbing his arm.

"Faith, It's ok. Do you want me to bring you home?" He placed a hand over hers suddenly feeling the need to take her from this place.

"No, I've got to get this cake done."

As if on cue the timer for the oven dinged.

Nodding his head he let go of her hand. "Ok, I'll see you."

Reluctantly she let go of his arm. "Thanks again, Jake."

"Faith, you can call me whenever. I'm still here. I'm not going anywhere." He gazed directly into her eyes then turned and walked from the room.

Jake was getting in his truck, when another set of headlights pulled up into the drive next to him.

"What are you doing here?" Evan called from his truck.

"I was just leaving. This place gives me the creeps." Jake cast a weary glance back towards the house.

"Yeah, it does that." Evan smirked following his gaze.

"If you're looking for Faith, she's inside."

"What happened? Door opened? Closed? Both?" Evan asked amused.

"Yeah, both."

Evan sat up, more serious. "Really? She see the ghost again?"

"Not this time. Apparently, she was seeing what the ghost wanted her to. I don't know." Frustrated, Jake ran a hand through his hair.

"Why are you here, Jake?" Evan asked gruffly.

"Because your sister called me," Jake snapped, narrowing his eyes at Evan. "Where were you?"

"Jake, this ain't high school," Evan growled through clenched teeth.

"No, Evan, it's not. If you haven't noticed we've all grown up. Maybe you should too." Jake slammed his door shut and started his truck.

CHAPTER 12

The days flew by. Friday was here. Faith paced her mother's kitchen nervously. She glanced at the rooster clock on the wall for the thousandth time before turning back toward the window.

"Would you sit down. You're wearing a hole in the floor," her father said from his spot at the kitchen table, pointing to the worn linoleum floor to make his point.

"Sorry, Dad. I'm just not good at waiting." She sighed, her gaze wandering back to the window.

"Well, you walkin' ain't gonna make the time go faster. What's wrong?" he asked warming his hands on the coffee mug in front of him.

"I just get nervous when the kids leave." The hands on the rooster clock ticked closer to her designated time to pick up the kids.

"You worried David won't take care of them?" It was a casual question, but Faith knew her dad well enough to know it was anything but.

"No, he's a good dad. He'll take care of them." Taking two steps back she leaned on the sink to peer out the window. *Breathe.* It's a beautiful day.

"There's more to being a dad than that." Grumbling her father smacked his cup down on the table.

"They'll be fine," she said turning back to her father, "I just can't stand not being there. You know."

"Humph." Her father didn't have to say what he was thinking.

"They'll be fine," Margaret chimed in from the laundry room, her coffee sitting cold on the table. Her mother seemed to be forever in motion, never sitting still. Must be where she got that from.

"I know that, but it doesn't stop me from worrying." Talking with her hands she paced back to the ticking clock.

"Make sure you take your phone. In case there's trouble."

"There shouldn't be any trouble, Dad. It's just dinner." *Tick. Tick. Tick.*

"Evan's worried about David wanting to have dinner with you," her mother said entering the kitchen in a waft of fabric softener and carrying a stack of folded dish cloths.

"Evan's worried?" Faith stopped her pacing to look at her mother for an explanation.

"I think it's odd, too. Him wanting to have dinner with you. He could have just picked up the kids like normal." Margaret shrugged placing the dish towels neatly in a drawer.

"Oh, it's probably just for the kids. I told you we're trying to not make this painful for them," Faith said reassuring herself.

"That's right," Margaret agreed. Her dad grumbled under his breath. She could imagine what he was thinking.

"Ok. I have my phone." Holding it up to show her dad, then slipping in it into her purse. "I'm going get the kids. I have their bags in the car."

"Maybe you should have asked someone to ride with you," her mother suggested bustling to the other cabinets and digging out a pot.

"Mom, please. I'm not going cross country."

Truth be told, she had considered asking Serena to come with her. Jake had crossed her mind too, more often than she cared to admit, but that was a whole different issue. That would be an awkward meal. The kids knew Serena and she probably would likely have agreed. The one thing that had stopped her was knowing David would flirt shamelessly, as was his habit when introduced to a beautiful woman. It was just easier to deal with David on her own and this way they could focus on the kids.

She had dressed casually since the restaurant the kids picked was one of those pizza arcades. Jeans and boots and her old faithful ponytail. She laughed at the thought of all the money she had spent over the years, coloring, shaping, and having her hair done. Somewhere along the way, the ponytail from her youth had made a comeback and now it was just the norm. She found it was just easier to pull her dark hair back than deal with it.

The drive was pleasant and they made good time. The kids' excited chatter kept her smiling and in a good mood. She only had a little work left to do on the cake, so she was trying to not stress over it.

She hadn't thought anything of David's offer for dinner until everyone else kept making a big deal out of it. Trying not to dwell on their suspicions, she kept the kids talking. Not a hard feat, all she had to do was mention the campout. That kept Trent talking until they pulled into the parking lot. David was there already waiting by the door. It did her heart good to see her children run to him and even more so to see he was just as excited to see them. If there was one thing she was thankful for in this ordeal, was that she knew he'd always be a dad to them no matter what. After hugging them for a few minutes, he straightened up and held out his arms to her. There were times like this when she looked at him and saw the boy she fell in love with. His dark hair always neatly trimmed and his perfect smile was hard to ignore.

"Hey, Faith. You look great."

Hugging him awkwardly, she smiled down at the kids, who were watching them with hope in their eyes. A familiar wave of guilt washed over her.

"Thanks. Been waiting long?"

"No. Just got here a few minutes ago. Ready guys?" He asked opening the door. Instantly they were assaulted by the sights and sounds from inside. Straight to the line to order food, then David took the kids to play games while Faith found them a table. While she waited for the pizza, she thought about the hug. It had been weird. Maybe it was all the talk about it before hand. Watching Hannah's excitement after winning a few tickets and David picking her up in a celebratory hug did funny things to her heart. Why were things so confusing?

The food was delivered and the kids came reluctantly to the table to eat.

"Come on guys. Let's eat and visit with Mom. Then we'll play some more," David urged, wrangling them to the table.

"Ok. Mom, did you see all my tickets?" Hannah asked proudly.

"I did. That is so awesome!"

"So, someone has a birthday coming up." David grinned at Trent taking a chair across from him. "What's it going to be this year, buddy?"

"I'm going to have a campout. Uncle Evan is going to help me. We get to sleep in a tent, and build a fire. It's gonna be great." The flow of words came out in the rush of one breath. In his excitement to tell his dad, Trent didn't catch the tightening of his father's jaw or the disappointment in his eyes.

"Wow, that sounds great. I didn't know you wanted to go camping. I can take you." Shrugging, David picked up a slice of pizza and took a bite.

"Yeah, Dad, could we? That would be awesome!" Following his dad's lead, Trent took a bite of pizza.

"Can I come too? Trent won't let me go to his party," Hannah pouted.

"We'll be there for the cake, Hannah, but the campout is just for the boys, remember?" Faith reminded her.

"Oh, I know, but Dad will take me too, right?" she asked looking up at her dad with hopeful eyes.

"Of course, honey." David patted Hannah's head then turning to Trent asked, "So where is Evan taking you?"

"Oh, it's going to be in the woods behind Miss Serena's house. She said we could go whenever we wanted, and her house is so cool. It's haunted. Mom saw a ghost."

Faith nearly choked on her soda. "What?"

She could tell by her son's face that the last bit of information had just slipped out in his excitement.

"I heard Uncle Evan and Maw Maw talking about it." He looked guilty down at his plate.

"It's ok. Let's talk about something else, please." Faith smiled to reassure him then turned back to her food.

David looked amused and asked Trent what kind of birthday presents he was wishing for, and that took them through the rest of the meal. As soon as they were done, the kids ran off to play games again. Instead of going with them, David came around the table and sat next to her.

"What's going on, Faith?" he asked.

"What are you talking about?" Stacking the plates, she gave him a weary glance.

"Ghosts? Evan taking him camping? Am I not even invited?" He reminded her of Hannah at that moment in full pout.

She blew out a breath. "David, he's been after me to go camping. Evan offered. I never know your schedule."

"Ahh... so you're punishing me," he accused.

"No, I am not. I just don't think you would be comfortable spending the night with my brother and a bunch of kids in a tent."

"Not exactly, but I'm his dad. I can take him camping," David argued.

"And I'm sure you will. It's not a onetime thing. You can take him whenever you want," she snapped.

"You know, Faith. This has been hard on me too. I miss you." His arm wrapped around her shoulders squeezing her to him.

"What are you doing?" She pushed him away, looking for the kids to make sure they weren't watching.

"Faith, I think we're making a mistake. I think you and the kids need to come home, where you belong."

At her stunned silence, he kept talking as if his words could magically erase the years of betrayal. She watched him, this man she had vowed to spend the rest of her life with and she realized she felt sorry for him. He honestly believed he could bully her into taking him back.

The glint in her eyes was just a flash, but it should have been a warning to him. "Are you serious?"

"Of course. Think about what you're doing to them. Moving them away from their family and friends."

"Wh-what I'm doing to them?" Sitting up straight in her chair, her voice rose a few octaves with her movement.

"Yeah, baseball is about to start. You know how much the team means to Trent. He won't be here to play." David was in full salesman mode. He would keep talking until she caved. Not this time.

She was thankful there were no utensils on the table to tempt her. Stabbing him in front of witnesses was not an option so she mangled her napkin instead. She smiled at him chanting to herself. *Breathe. Breathe.* When she thought she could refrain from hurting him, she spoke softly.

"First of all, they are with family. My family, who they barely ever got to see while we were married because it was inconvenient for you. Your family can see them whenever they want. I would never keep them, or you, for that matter, from seeing the kids." Slapping a hand over his mouth when he tried to speak again, Faith continued, "Secondly, our son hates baseball. It means a lot to you. It was important to you that he played on your team. He was miserable, but you never wanted to see it."

The shock on his face almost made her stop there, but she knew she'd never be able to live with herself unless she made it crystal clear to him how she felt. She would never pretend again for anyone's sake.

"I am exactly where I belong. If you had wanted me, I would have never left. You just wanted the status of marriage and the idea of the stability of a family, but you never wanted to be in a committed relationship."

Her voice lowered dangerously as she got in his face. "How dare you try to use the kids to guilt me!"

David shifted away from her in surprise, holding his hands up in surrender. "I'm sorry. I didn't mean it like that. I just want to make sure this is what you want, and it's what's best for the kids."

"Best for the kids? Now you're worried about what's best for the kids?"

"Faith, please." He grabbed for her hand.

"No, David. It's not going to happen." She pushed him away again, and got up to find her kids.

Trent was playing a video game while Hannah cheered him on.

"Hey guys. If y'all are good, I'm going to head home, ok?" she asked.

Hannah immediately hugging her waist whined, "Can't you stay, Mom?"

"Only a few more games." She smiled down at her daughter. This was so hard. When she looked up, David had joined them and was watching her closely. Walking up he pulled her and Hannah into a group hug.

Whispering into her ear, "You know you can stay the weekend with us. I'm making pancakes for breakfast."

Hissing, she pushed him away. The devilish grin on his face was one Faith knew too well. It was the look he got when he thought he was getting away with something.

"No, I can't. I have a cake to finish and I have work," she said firmly. "In fact, you guys give me a hug. I need to get back." She hugged and kissed them both. David was waiting patiently for his turn. She rolled her eyes at him, but he pulled her to him anyway.

"You can always change your mind. I'll see you Sunday when I bring them back," he said kissing her cheek.

"Yeah, see you guys on Sunday. Be good for Daddy." She smiled at her kids, then sent David one last glare before she stomped off.

What the hell was he up to? Fuming, she thought about it all the way back to Cypress Point. Driving straight to Serena's, she planned to finish the cake. Faith was disappointed and a little nervous to find that Serena wasn't there. Focusing on the cake, she went about her work, finishing quickly. She was boxing it up when her phone buzzed.

A text from Claire. **Come meet us @the bar. Waiting for you.**

She was still steamed about David's behavior and a drink sounded great to her. Why not? She'd been thinking about Jake a lot too. She used to love to hear him sing and he'd been so good to her since the flat. He kept coming around to check up on her and their talk at the barn had made her feel better. She still wasn't sure why she called him of all people when the weird stuff happened. Remembering the fuzzy feeling and the music, she looked around uncomfortably. She quickly wiped down the counter and made sure everything was put away then clicked off the kitchen light. She thought about running through the foyer, but decided a fast walk would do. As she passed the mirror, she couldn't help but look into it. Relieved when she saw only herself looking back at her. Turning it over in her mind trying to figure out what triggered it, she stopped at the door, listening.

There was only silence. The house felt at peace. Sighing with relief she locked the door behind her.

CHAPTER 13

She wasn't coming. Jake had been watching the door all night. *You fool*, he cursed himself. She's with him. Faith's little announcement had stung more than he cared to admit. *I'm having dinner with David.* Asshole. Still a tiny bit of him, well maybe more than tiny, was holding out hope for them. There was no way she'd go back to that asshole. Not the Faith he knew.

He was amused to see Claire show up with Evan in tow. Remembering his manners, he decided to say hello and thank them for coming out. It wasn't all manners. He was curious to see what Evan would say, and if they would have any news about Faith. Like maybe she changed her mind, or wasn't having dinner with the creep.

"Hey guys, glad you could make it." Jake crossed the dance floor to greet Claire and Evan.

"We wouldn't have missed it. Right Evan?" Claire's blue eyes moved anxiously from Jake to Evan.

"Yeah, sure." His voice dripping with sarcasm, Evan wrapped a possessive arm around Claire, who elbowed him softly in the stomach. Sighing heavily he continued, "Nah, really. I've been telling Claire about Amy. We've been wanting to catch a show."

Amy LeBlue had a popular local band that usually packed the house at any location. Tonight was already promising to be another full house. With the weather finally straightening out, people were ready to get out and about.

They made small talk mostly about music and the band. Jake quickly realized Evan was avoiding the subject of Faith.

"Hey Jake!" Jake recognized the sickly sweet voice before the hand rubbed his arm.

"Hey Tracey," he said without turning.

Jake knew the moment she noticed Evan, her voice almost became a purr.

"Oh my God, Evan is that you?" Tracey's hand abandoned Jake's arm to snake up Evan's.

Evan's dark eyes narrowed, "Tracey. I don't know if you've met my girlfriend, Claire. She teaches at the school." Evan maneuvered Claire from his side to stand directly in front of him, his arms hugging her from behind. Claire, blushing prettily, smiled at Tracey.

"Um, no. I don't think so." Tracey gave Claire a half smile, immediately turning her attention back to Jake. "So, how about we get a drink before the band starts, and then maybe after...." She let the suggestion hang.

"No, thanks. I'm not drinking tonight. I don't wanna sound sloppy." Jake grinned at her.

"After then?" She raised an eyebrow and licked her lips. The blood red nails gripping his arm again.

"No, I'm waiting for someone." He gave her a pointed look, the smile gone from his face. Once spoken, he realized how true his words were. He was waiting. Waiting for Faith. She might not show tonight, but he'd still be waiting. He felt sorry for Tracey. She was a bar fly, another lonely soul passing the time, just like he had been.

"Oh." Snatching her hand away and resting it on her hip, she glared at Jake. "See ya around then."

After she stalked away, Claire asked, "Who was that?"

"Nobody." Jake and Evan answered at the same time. Looking at each other they both grinned. Jake catching the look on Claire's face decided that was probably a conversation he didn't need to be involved in, so he took his leave.

"I'll let you two find a table. I've got to get ready." He made his way back to the stage, glancing back at the door, still hoping Faith would show.

The first set flew by, the band and the crowd warming up to each other. Hiding his disappointment he lost himself in the music. The notes and melody gave him something to focus on, adding his voice when needed.

Amy had been a good friend over the years and at one time they had even danced around a possible relationship. But playing music, keeping a band together, and the call of the road didn't make for an ideal relationship. At least not for him. She had wanted Jake to go with her. He wouldn't go. He loved music, but he knew his home was here. And she wasn't Faith. It would have never lasted. So they had remained friends, Jake sitting in whenever he could. They were both happy with the arrangement.

Amy smiled across the makeshift stage at him as the song ended and gave him a nod. That was the hand off. He gave her a wink and nodded to the band to start the next song. As if by magic, Faith appeared at the edge of the dancefloor. He didn't know how long she had been there. The crowd had grown so much he had lost sight of the door. It didn't matter. She was here now. Not with David, but here with him.

So he sang his song, a song he knew by heart, a club favorite. This time he sang to her. To the young girl that had stolen his heart so many years ago. He knew he had been waiting for this moment. Every other time he had played this song before, had been a rehearsal for this. All the hurt, all the longing, every bit of sorrow he felt over the years was poured out into the song. His soul bared for all to hear, but no one else mattered. It was Faith he sang to. When the song ended, he had to compose himself. Putting down his guitar, he walked off the stage. He heard Amy announcing they were going to take a break as he walked out into the cool night air.

Hearing the door open and close again Jake knew Amy had followed him out.

"Jake, that was so intense. Are you ok?" Amy's worried voice sounded in the darkness.

"Yeah, I just needed to get that out." Jake took a few steps, breathing in the fresh air.

"Wow! Well, you did it, my friend. I had to take a break. You had me almost in tears. I don't know if I can follow that act. You trying to show me up?" she asked jokingly punching him in the arm.

"No, it's something I need to work out, obviously."

"Hey, it's a chick? It'll be alright. Come here." Amy opening her arms wrapped him in a warm hug.

Faith watched Jake stride off of the stage through blurry eyes. The back door slammed behind him and her vision wavered. *Breathe. Breathe.* She had been so entranced in the song that she had forgotten to breathe. The crowd pushed into her, shoving her on to the dance floor. *Breathe. Breathe.* Making her way anxiously to the back door, she needed air and she needed to see Jake. The heavy back door opened into the darkness and the quiet fresh air. Faith breathed in as her eyes adjusted, taking in Jake and Amy in each other's arms.

"Oh...I'm sorry. I didn't mean to interrupt." She gulped at the air. *Breathe. Breathe.*

"No, you didn't." Amy stepped back looking from Faith to Jake. "This is her, right?"

"Who?" Faith asked.

"The one he's been singing to all these years. I'm glad you were finally here to hear it." Amy gave Jake a knowing smile, "Take your time. I've got you covered."

The hazy light from inside cast a glow into the darkness as she opened the door and disappeared back inside. Faith and Jake stood in the darkness.

"Jake?" Faith was unsure of what to say.

"How was dinner?" His voice sounded strained.

"Glad it's over," Faith snorted trying to lighten the mood.

"Faith, I can't pretend anymore." Faith was caught off guard by his words. His words that mirrored her own thoughts just a few hours earlier.

"If you're going back to him, I need to know. I can't..." his voice trailed off. The emotion in it hurt her.

"No. Jake, I'm not going anywhere." Faith reached for him instinctively wanting to comfort him as he had been comforting her the past few weeks. Just like the song, his arms were home and always would be. His mouth found hers, desperately seeking confirmation of feelings returned and she answered in kind. The need exploded through them.

Pulling his head back to look into her eyes. "Damn, girl. That's a relief."

"What?" she asked huskily.

"That nothing has changed." His arms tightened around her.

"Of course things have changed." Faith looked up at him wishing she could see the warm color of his eyes in the darkness.

"No, not how I feel about you. Not how I feel when I'm with you. I still want you Faith. After all of these years I was afraid I had just built up the memory of you to drive myself crazy." His hands found the back pockets of her jeans and slipped inside to cup her closer. Drawing their hips together, Faith could feel his arousal. She welcomed the warmth of desire his touch ignited within her.

For one delicious moment, this was all that existed. Then the reality of the situation and all the complications came crashing down on her. "We were just kids, too young to know what we really wanted." Faith shook her head sadly.

"We're not kids anymore, and here we are." He shrugged his shoulders under her arms, still wrapped around his neck.

"Oh, Jake," she said putting her head to his chest, "if only we could go back."

"No, there's no going back. We've got right now and everything in front of us. Please say there's hope for us," he whispered into her neck.

"Jake I'm a mess right now." Her conscious was battling with desire. She didn't want anyone to get hurt. She had her kids to think about and her family.

"All I'm asking for is an answer. Tell me, am I crazy for waiting?" She could hear the desperation in his voice, and it washed all doubts away. To be able to feel again was like a breath of fresh air.

"No." Her hands framed his face as she reached up to kiss him again. The heat rose like a wave and carried them until he had her backed against the building. He picked her up and she wrapped her legs around him. Running her hands through his hair and then pulling at his shirt as he ground himself against her.

The creak of the door opening stopped them both cold. When the light and noise from inside didn't go away, he let her slide back down to the ground as he reluctantly let her go.

"Faith?" A female voice called.

"Yeah, Claire. I'm here," Faith answered from the darkness trying to smooth her sweater back into place.

"Oh. Evan's been looking for you." Claire grimaced when she noticed Jake.

"Of course," Faith said rolling her eyes, "Tell him I'm fine."

"Yeah, he was worried about David." Claire looked nervously over her shoulder.

Evan's form filled the open doorway blocking out the hazy light from inside.

"Worried about David or about me?" Jake asked Evan directly.

"Humph. Maybe both," Evan grumbled.

"Evan don't," Faith warned.

"I just wanted to make sure that asshole didn't try anything. I don't trust him."

Jake stood straighter taking a step towards Evan. "What?"

"Not you, asshole. The other one," he snapped at Jake then turned back to his sister, "I can see you're fine." Then added to Claire, "Come on Darlin'. I feel like dancing."

"Wait a minute. You're just going to walk away?" Jake asked as if daring him.

"Yep. I am. I said I feel like dancing, and you're not exactly light on your feet." He held out a hand to Claire, pulling her close when she took hold and nudged her towards the door. "You kids behave yourselves. We'll chat later."

Faith stood in stunned silence as the door closed again leaving them in darkness.

"Who was that? And what did he do with my brother?"

"I think your friend may have something to do with his change of heart," Jake said grinning at her. "So, do you want to go back in?"

"Don't you have to?"

"That's the beauty of sitting in. They don't really need you," he laughed. "What do you say we pretend like we are teenagers again and fog up the windows of my truck?"

Even though he couldn't see her face that well in the dark she felt the blush on her cheeks.

"Faith?" he asked nervously.

She grabbed his hand, and pulled him towards the parking lot and into the light, her dark eyes shining with mischief.

"You're the one that said we can't go back. I have a better idea. Follow me."

CHAPTER 14

Faith woke slowly. The music. Ugh. The melody flowed through her, bringing her close to consciousness then pushing her back into sleep. Floating back and forth, she felt the arm around her and smiled. Snuggling closer to the warm naked body next to her, she drifted off again.

The melody repeated over and over. She groaned. No kids. She didn't need to be up this early. Opening her eyes slowly, she glanced at Jake, who slept soundly. She should at least let Serena know they were here. She must have gotten home after they did. They had been a little too preoccupied to notice. Wow, after all these years. Her and Jake. How sweet, and hot it had been. She had needed to see him after dinner with David. As persuasive as her husband could be, she knew she could never go back to the empty existence they had shared.

Quietly slipping out of bed and padding down the hallway, she went in search of Serena.

Seeing Jake on stage last night had warmed her heart. The music seemed to come from him. His talent had always awed her. Then he had started to sing, a song she knew, but it had mesmerized her. Faith knew he had been singing to her, and the depth of emotion that had come from him had also stirred and released something that she had buried long ago. Her feelings for him. The love of a young girl that was so strong and pure, it hurt to remember, but she knew he was remembering too. It had shattered her and freed her at the same time. How could she have ever mistaken what she had with David for that. She had always chalked up the fond memories to being young and naive.

Not finding Serena upstairs, she went down the staircase. As she descended the music grew louder and her vision became blurry.

"Oh no. No. Not again."

Glancing in the mirror when she reached the foyer she was shocked. The young woman she had seen before looked back at her. Her glowing face, rumpled from sleep, shone with hope. Her dark hair hung loose to the shoulder of her white cotton gown.

The music pulled her towards the parlor. A loud voice violently thundered over the music. She couldn't make out the muffled and incoherent words, but the intent was unmistakable. She peered around the corner into the parlor and her heart fell. A large man stood looking down over a boy sprawled and unmoving on the floor. No, the figure on the floor was young but he was a man. He was familiar to her judging by the flood of love she felt gazing at him. Her love was overcome by terror, seeing the rage of the older man with blood on his hands. She screamed and the man turned towards her, his face filled with anger and disgust.

Frightened she ran back to the stairs, her bare feet catching on the hem of her nightgown as she tried to climb the steps. Pain shot through her as her shin banged the edge of a step and she scrambled frantically up the staircase on her hands and knees. Running the rest of the way to her room she slammed the door behind her, and huddled against the wall. Praying to God, she waited. The door opened, the giant figure filling the doorway. He stood there at first in silence radiating anger.

Then in a low and threatening voice that seemed to reach across the room and deflate any and all hope she had of happiness he said, "Never again. Never again."

The door banged shut and she heard the key in the lock. Sobbing to herself she listened to the heavy footsteps make their way back down the stairs. Hearing muffled shouts, she pulled herself up by the window sill to look out. Watching in horror as the large man dragged the limp body from the porch and head towards the woods. Screaming, she beat her hands on the cold glass, "No, Poppa, no!"

Warm hands and a soft familiar voice woke her from the nightmare.

"Faith? Babe, it's ok. I'm here." Jake watching her with concern, rubbed her arms gently.

"Jake," Faith gasped for air looking around wildly, her hands fisted against his chest. "Did I hit you?" she asked horrified.

"It's ok. That must have been some doozy of a dream." He wiped at her tear stained face.

"I'm not so sure it was a dream," she said, the sadness still weighing her down, and her shin still throbbing.

"What are you talking about?" Jake shifted to sit up in the bed, pulling the sheet with his movement and uncovering Faith's breasts. She looked around confused. There was no way she went downstairs naked. She remembered the white cotton gown and the feel of it next to her skin.

"It was her. I was her." Faith pulled the sheet back over her nakedness.

"Like before?"

"I have to find Scrcna." Faith sat up pulling the sheet around her.

"Right now? Faith, this is crazy." He tried to pull her back to him using the sheet.

"I heard the music again." She yanked the sheet free from his hands.

Jake froze as she pushed away from the bed. "Music?"

"Yeah, like before, the same song. I thought I heard it on the radio and that's why it was in my head but now I don't know. I think it has something to do with her." Noticing Jake's serious expression she asked, "What's wrong?"

"Music. I had a dream about music, too."

"Really?" She jumped back onto the bed. "Sing it to me."

"I don't know. Hang on." Throwing his legs over the side of the bed, he put his hands to his head, trying to remember.

A soft knock at the door startled them both.

"Hey guys, it's me. I heard hollering, slamming doors, and footsteps. Everything ok in there?" Serena's worried voice asked from the other side of the door.

"Yeah, I think so. Give me a minute and I'll meet you downstairs," Faith answered.

"Ok, I'll put the coffee on." Serena's voice sounded muffled as she moved away from the door.

Kneeling behind Jake on the bed, she rubbed his shoulders.

"Do you remember? Maybe I can hum it to you," she said trying to recall the melody. Bits of the dream flashed through her mind filling her with dread.

"I can't remember it now, but I will, eventually." He turned toward her, pulling her into his lap. Faith wrapped her arms around him and snuggled closer. "You ok? I never believed much in this kind of stuff, but it's kinda freaking me out."

"Yeah, me too, the ghost lead us to that sign for a reason. She wanted us to find it. I'm thinking she's trying to tell us something and not just the name of the house."

CHAPTER 15

Jake took his time dressing trying to remember the dream. This was too weird. Finally being with Faith after so long had definitely been worth the wait. The ghost stuff had him freaked out and a little jumpy. That had to be it. He hated seeing her like that. The crying and confusion wasn't like her at all. She had been so distraught it had broken his heart. However, it had definitely boosted his ego knowing he had made her forget the cake, work and even the kids for a little while.

Kids. Could he even handle that? Of course he could. He loved kids. That was stupid. Why was he even thinking about this? Because he knew he wanted Faith forever, and that meant her kids too. What if they didn't like him? He shook off the feeling of doom that had suddenly settled over him and tried again to remember the dream. Why couldn't he remember? There was music. He tried to grasp at the wisps of the dream, only to find it gone again. Was it him singing to her last night? Thinking about it, he willed it to jog his memory, but that didn't seem familiar, either.

In the kitchen, he found Serena scribbling wildly in her notebook at the counter and Faith pacing with her coffee mug.

"Tell me again. You went downstairs?" Serena peered at Faith from her perch at the counter island.

"No, I thought I had, but when I woke up I was still in bed with Jake." Faith glanced at him shyly.

"The best way to wake up if you ask me," he teased enjoying the blush on her cheeks. "Of course, I wouldn't be telling anybody about the tears. I've got a reputation to protect."

"So it was more like a dream or an out of body experience?" Serena asked ignoring Jake's attempt at humor.

"Out of body?" Faith put her cup down. "That sounds scary."

"Well, wasn't it?" Serena asked.

"I was terrified. It was me, but I was her. This sounds insane." Faith smoothed back her hair and pulled on her pony tail.

"You looked in the mirror, and it was her?" Serena tapped her pen against the notebook.

"Yes."

"The parlor, was it like it is now or like before?" Serena asked in a businesslike manner. *Tap. Tap. Tap.*

"Before. I was scared. That man. I was afraid of him. I knew he would hurt me and I was terrified for the boy. I loved him." Faith clutched at her sweater.

Jake's stomach knotted at her admission.

"But it was her, right? She loved him," Serena tried to clarify.

"Yes, she did, but I felt it." Pointing to her chest, Faith paced again.

Serena eyed them both. "You went to the front bedroom upstairs where Jake found you the other day? Not the bedroom y'all slept in last night."

"Yeah."

"And it looked the same as it did then?" The tapping stopped as Serena began writing again. Jake watched them both amazed but suddenly uncomfortable.

"Oh, yes, it was my... I mean her room. She was trying to get away from that man. She felt safe there. But the man came and locked her in. She was devastated, she couldn't get to the boy to help him. She was so afraid that her father would hurt him."

"Her father?" Serena stopped writing and looked at Faith.

"Yeah, it felt like it." Faith's ponytail bobbed as she nodded her head.

"That's what you were screaming when I tried to wake you." Jake said softly remembering her desperate cries. "No Poppa no, something like that." He didn't know why but suddenly he felt like he couldn't breathe.

"I'm so glad you were here." Serena went back to scribbling.

"Me, too," Jake said trying to shake off the strange feeling that someone was watching him. "Coffee?"

"Yes, I'm sorry." Faith got him a mug and poured without thinking.

"I can do that. We're not at the diner." Jake took the cup from her.

"Jake, Faith mentioned you were dreaming too? Something about music," Serena asked curiously.

"I can't remember. It's driving me nuts." He sat at the counter running a hand through his hair. "But what are the odds we were dreaming the same thing, right?"

"Anything is possible and I'm not so sure it was a dream," Serena said simply.

"Who are you?" Jake asked before he could stop himself.

Faith choked on her coffee and Serena just smiled at him.

"You know my name. You know this is my home. What exactly are you asking me?" Dark eyes regarded him patiently waiting for more questions.

"Jake don't be rude. I'd expect that from Evan, not you," Faith hissed at him.

"Sorry, I'm just a little freaked out by all of this and you seem to be taking it in stride like it's a normal everyday occurrence." He realized as soon as he said it, that it was. "It is, isn't it? None of this shocks you?"

"Shock, no, but the frequency and the intensity is surprising. This is not a normal occurrence, even for me." She shrugged, pushing her dark curls off of her neck then picked up the notebook again. "I wish you could remember. If you do, you'll tell me or Faith, right?"

"Yeah, sure." The uncomfortable feeling grew. Gulping his coffee, he stood. "I've got to go."

"I'll walk you out," Faith said grabbing his hand. She seemed as anxious for him to leave as he was. He waited until they were out on the porch before he spoke. "Faith, this is weird. I don't like you being here."

"What?"

"If it only happens here, then don't come here. Something is wrong with this place. I don't like it." Shaking his head, Jake looked back into the foyer nervously.

"I have to come here, and sometimes I am by myself. It doesn't happen all the time. Once we figure out what she's trying to tell us, she'll leave us alone. I think," Faith tried to reassure him.

Jake didn't realize she had stopped talking at first, he was too busy gazing at the sign by the door. Coeur du Bayou. It seemed so familiar to him, the sign, Faith standing in doorway, and the feeling that something terrible was going to happen.

"Where did this come from?" he asked not taking his eyes from it.

"Oh, that's the sign we found. I told you about that. She wanted us to find it. Serena thinks she wanted us to know the house's name."

He touched the sign, tracing the fancy lettering with his fingertip.

"Is something wrong?"

"No, I'm glad you found it. It's pretty, but something about it makes me sad too."

"Really? Maybe I should get Serena." Faith turned back towards the door.

"No." He grabbed her arm and pulled her close making her giggle.

"Ok, I'll tell her later." Faith wrapped her arms around his neck.

"Yeah, I'll see you at the diner." He bent his head to hers and she met him the rest of the way. The kiss was warm and hungry and left them both wanting.

As he drove away, Jake started humming a melody that seemed so familiar, but he couldn't place it. Suddenly in a hurry to get home, he hummed and hummed willing himself to not lose it.

CHAPTER 16

"One special and one cheeseburger with Cajun fries." Faith smiled at the older couple as she placed their orders in front of them. Helen and George were regulars. They showed up almost every Saturday night. Their date night. Faith thought it was the cutest thing. Helen had been the Postmaster as long as she could remember and George had owned the feed store. Now retired, he spent most of his time building custom bird houses and carving lifelike duck decoys.

"I keep telling him he shouldn't be eating like a teenager. It's going to catch up with him," Helen clucked.

"My stomach doesn't know any better." George smiled patting her hand.

"It's not your stomach I'm worried about. If you could see what that stuff is doing to your arteries, you'd think twice." Helen wagged a finger at him.

Faith laughed as she put more napkins on the table. "Y'all enjoy. Holler if you need anything."

The bell on the door jingled as she made her way around the counter. Smiling hopefully, she turned expecting to see Jake.

"Oh, it's you, Claire," she said not bothering to hide her disappointment.

"Don't sound so excited," Claire pouted.

"Sorry. I've just been waiting on Jake. He said he'd see me for supper, and he hasn't showed up yet. I hope everything's ok." Faith looked past her friend to the window outside, hoping to see Jake's truck.

"I'm sure it is. Last night was... good?" Claire's blush made Faith laugh.

"Yes, it was." Faith smiled sheepishly.

"The cake?" Claire prompted.

"Was awesome! They loved it. I'm just glad I got it there in one piece." Faith had been thrilled with the response of her customer. Happy customers would hopefully turn into recommendations and more happy customers.

"The kids?" Claire leaned against the counter hugging her purse to her.

"Still with their dad. He'll bring them home tomorrow." Faith rolled her eyes and sighed. She was not looking forward to seeing David again so soon.

"Was it weird?" Claire whispered, "We haven't really had a chance to talk."

"Yeah, I think he was hurt that Trent wants to have a campout with Evan for his birthday." Glancing around the diner, she remembered

Tracey and one of her minions were in a booth and appeared to be terribly interested in their conversation. Turning her back towards them she lowered her voice. "He asked me to go back home."

Claire's huge blue eyes widened even more as she put a hand over her mouth and whispered, "What about Jake?"

"This isn't about Jake. I'm not going back. I should have never married David, but I did. He doesn't really want to be married anyway. I think it was what was expected of him. Who knows?" she said shrugging her shoulders. Then she thought of Claire's talent for spilling the beans. "Don't tell anyone. Especially Evan."

Claire looked down sheepishly. "I won't. I promise. I said I was sorry about all of that."

"I know. It's ok. Is Evan still mad at me?"

Claire giggled. "I think he's getting over it. We actually talked about it," she said excitedly.

"He asked you?" Faith squeaked.

"Oh, no. We talked about kids. You know I'm not getting any younger and I don't have a lot of time, but we both want kids." She grinned at Faith, her eyes twinkling.

"The lunkhead needs to ask you to marry him first," Faith snorted shaking her head.

The bell from the order window dinged.

"Got those orders ready, Faith," Gil called from the kitchen.

"Got it!" she answered. "That's probably yours," she told Claire as she went to retrieve the food containers and bag them. "Yes it is."

As she rang up the ticket, she thought about the night before and Evan's reaction to finding her with Jake. Whispering over the register to Claire, "So what did Evan say about me and Jake? I can't believe he didn't blow a fuse."

"We've talked about it, after that day at your mom's. I just reminded him that you are a grown up now and he can't tell you who to date." Claire shrugged like it had been an easy feat.

"I'm sure that went over well." Faith rolled her eyes trying to imagine Evan not bossing her around.

"Not really, but he did get this weird look on his face and said he'd butt out. He was just worried about you. Jake kinda has a reputation with the women, and he didn't want you getting hurt. You haven't been around, so you might not know." Claire glanced over in Tracey's direction as she dug through her purse, pulling out her wallet.

"Oh. I think we're good," Faith said slowly.

"I'm sure. After last night, that song. Oh my God, Faith. I just about cried. That was incredibly romantic and Evan...." she put her hand to her chest. "That seemed to take away any doubt he had."

"Really?" Faith smiled remembering. She had been so mesmerized by his voice and emotion that she hadn't thought to look at anyone else. In fact, the whole room had seemed to vanish. Her eyes started to water. "It was great, wasn't it?"

"It was awesome. I'm so sorry Serena wasn't there." Counting out the bills, Claire stopped and sighed heavily.

"I know, and I forgot to tell her this morning."

"We can get together later if you want. Evan will be working," Claire suggested.

"No, thanks. Jake is supposed to meet me." Taking the money Claire handed her, she made change. "But I promise we'll get together soon. I need to check on my customers."

"Ok, yeah. Tomorrow?"

"See you." She watched Claire leave then before she could ask if anyone needed anything, Tracey and her minion made their way to the register.

"We're done," Tracey said waving the bill at her.

"Ok, I'll ring you guys up." Faith held out her hand for the bill, dreading the encounter. Tracey had never been a pleasant person.

"Separately," snapped Tracey's minion. Definitely cut from the same cloth, her over painted face, freshly dyed hair and bedazzled clothing couldn't hide the years spent hanging out in smoky bar rooms. Faith didn't remember her name but she knew she wasn't as old as she looked or as young as she dressed.

"Of course." Faith smiled at her.

"You waiting on Jake?" Tracey asked with a glint in her eye.

"Umm...Yes, actually I am. He's usually here for supper," Faith said trying to sound casual.

"Well, I wouldn't wait up for him." The blonde purred like a cat waiting to pounce.

Faith cursed herself for taking the bait. "Why is that?"

"Cause Amy's been there all day," Tracey blurted out with a giggle.

"Oh." *Breathe. Breathe.*

"Yeah, you know, she stays there sometimes when she's in town for a gig." She turned to her minion adding, "You'd think she'd get a hotel room, big star and all. Jake's not much of a housekeeper, you know. I guess it's a bachelor thing. I tried straightening up for him some when I stayed over, but you know men. They don't care about that stuff."

"No, I guess they don't," Faith said handing her the receipt. "Have a good night."

"Yeah you too, Honey." Tracey gave her a full smile before she headed for the door.

Faith stood frozen as the door closed behind them. The jingling of the bell seemed to echo through the almost empty restaurant. *Breathe. Breathe.* Forcing herself to move, she started to clear their table, stacking the dishes together more forcefully than normal. She glanced over to see Helen and George watching her.

"Sorry." She gave them a small smile.

"Don't you listen to a word that girl said. She is a malicious gossip and she's been after Jake for a while now, and only because no one else in town will look twice at her," Helen tried to comfort her.

"But Jake does?" Faith plopped into the booth miserably.

"Oh no. He talks to her because he talks to everyone. He's friendly like that. He's always been that way." Helen smiled kindly and George nodded his head in agreement.

"So, she's never slept over and straighten his house?" Faith wondered out loud.

Helen blushed and George looked down at his empty plate. "Well, I don't know anything about that, but I wouldn't listen to her. You need to talk to Jake. She's just jealous."

Faith shook her head sighing, then gathering up the plates she headed to the kitchen. Gil had already started the cleanup.

"You ok?" he asked without looking at her.

"Yeah, I'm fine." She scraped the food from the plates and put them in the sink to rinse.

"Hey, don't take it out on my dishes," he said finally looking at her. "You're not ok. You can cry if you need to. I'll go take care of the love birds." He smiled sadly at her then turned to walk out.

"Gil?" Her eyes burned with mad tears as he turned back to her. "Did he? I mean.... Tracey? Amy?"

"Damn it. I told him this would happen." Gil hung his head unable to meet her eyes.

"Told him what would happen?" She leaned on the sink bracing herself for the answer.

"That he would hurt you. Not on purpose, but it was bound to happen." He shrugged, shaking his head sadly.

"Take me there," she ordered, pushing herself away from the sink.

"What? Where?" Gil fidgeted nervously pulling at his stained apron.

"Take me by his house. I need to see, but I don't want to go alone," Faith pleaded with him.

"No, Faith. You don't need to see. Helen's right. Don't listen to that skank. Wait until you've calmed down. Like tomorrow.... or Monday. However long you need, then talk to him." He waved his arms as he spoke reminding Faith of a large bird trying to take flight.

"Fine." She shook her head and turned back to the sink of dishes. Once he had left the room, she found her cell phone and dialed Claire's number.

"Hey what's up?" Faith could hear Rosie whining in the background when Claire answered.

"Is Evan gone?" she asked quickly.

"Yeah. You want me to call him and tell him to go by there?" Claire offered.

"No, I need for you to drive me somewhere." Faith watched Gil talking with Helen and George through the order window.

"I thought you had plans?" Claire's voice sounded far away and muffled.

"Plans change. I need someone to ride with me. I don't want to go to jail today. Give me fifteen minutes to clean this up, and be waiting for me out front in your car," Faith said hoping she'd agree.

"Ok, I'll be waiting."

Faith pressed the end button before she could say anything else. The jingle of the front door told her the last of the customers had left and Gil was coming back to the kitchen.

She needed to know. She wouldn't be played for a fool again and Faith didn't think her heart could survive if Jake betrayed it. All of her hopes rested on that trust.

CHAPTER 17

Claire was waiting just like she promised. Faith was not surprised when she saw Serena riding shotgun.

"I guess I should have said it was top secret." Faith sent a glare to the back of Claire's head as she slipped into the backseat.

"I figured we might need back up." Claire grinned over her shoulder at her. "I don't want to go to jail either."

"I am intrigued. Should I have brought the bolt cutters?" Serena teased Claire. The blush on Claire's face told Faith she was remembering the night she met Evan.

"No, I don't think so," Faith said miserably.

"Where are we going?" Claire turned in her seat to look at Faith.

"Jake's. Do you know where he lives?" Faith leaned forward grabbing onto the seat in front of her. At her serious tone, both of her friends sat up straighter.

"No." Claire bit her lip and glanced hesitantly at Serena.

"Well, apparently you may be the only female in town that doesn't." Faith flung herself back against the seat and took a deep breath.

"Huh?" Claire asked confused.

Serena hissed out a breath. "If it makes you feel any better, I don't either."

"Slightly better. Let me drive," Faith said getting back out of the car.

"I don't understand." Claire shook her head as Faith opened the driver door. "Everything was great not even an hour ago."

"That skank was listening to our convo and informed me that Jake has had female company all day. And it's a frequent occurrence with more than one woman, including herself."

"She's just jealous." Claire got out of the car to let Faith drive. "She was there last night, and I promise you it killed her to see Jake singing to you," she added over the back seat as Faith started the car.

"Maybe. I don't know." Faith thought back to what Helen said.

"And for what purpose are we heading to his house?" Serena asked carefully.

"I need to see if it's true." Faith hated to admit it, but it was the truth. She was not about to guess and hope her way through another relationship. She needed to know.

"And if she's not there?" Serena arched an eyebrow at her.

Faith thought it over. If Amy wasn't there, she'd feel stupid. "We leave and get some wine." She smiled over at Serena.

"If she is?" Serena smiled back at her.

"We slash their tires, then leave and get some tequila." She'd feel stupid either way, there was no easy way around it.

Serena laughed and Claire sat in the back seat quietly, a worried expression on her face.

"What Claire?" Faith regarded Claire in the rear view mirror.

"Nothing."

"Did you tell Evan?" Faith narrowed her eyes accusingly.

"No, I didn't." Claire shook her head and sighed.

"Did you tell my mom?" Faith asked only half joking.

"Of course not." Claire crossed her arms in a huff obviously offended.

"Then what's wrong with you? You look like you're about to cry." Faith glanced at her again in the mirror becoming concerned.

"I just don't understand." Claire uncrossed her arms to talk with her hands then pointed to herself for emphasis. "I was there. He meant it. Even Evan thought so."

"Maybe he's made a habit out of singing to women in bars and he's just so good at it, it fooled us all," Faith spat out. *Breathe. Breathe.* She knew she shouldn't be so mad. She had left. There had to be others. Her reasoning didn't stop the hurt or the anger she felt.

"Faith, for whatever it's worth, I've seen him with you. I know he cares. That's not an act," Serena tried to reassure her.

"Hmmph," Faith snorted.

They were all quiet as Faith drove them out of town. She knew the dirt roads were unfamiliar to her passengers, but she knew them well. Getting closer to the barn, her eyes watered as she thought of all the times they had met in secret. They had been young and madly in love. She had lost her virginity in that barn with Jake. She remembered the sweet rushed urgency of that awkward first tryst, then his tender words just this morning. Had it been an act?

Keeping her eyes on the road in front of her, she chanted to herself to breathe. She would know one way or the other soon enough. The old farm house had been in his family for years. No one was surprised when he ended up there. His brothers, the ones that stayed to farm, had all married young and built their own homes. How ironic that she had once hoped they would live there together and have a family of their own.

Breathe. Breathe. Straining to see in the darkness, she pulled off the road before the long drive way.

"I don't see anything," Claire's worried voice sounded from the back seat when Faith turned off the car.

"I'm not going to drive right up to the house."

"Why not?" Claire peered out of the car window into the darkness.

"Claire, it's just a little ways. We'll be ok," Faith tried to reassure her friend, "Come on, or don't. Stay here if you want," Faith added with a shrug.

Unsure, Claire glanced at Serena, then back at Faith. "I'm coming."

"Ok, I'll use my phone for a light, so we can see where we're walking." Faith shut the car door softly and waited for Claire to get out, making sure she didn't slam her door.

"What exactly are we looking for?" Serena asked following Faith's lead and closed her door quietly.

"See those lights." Faith pointed to a glow out in the darkness. "That's the house over there."

"Once we see if her car is there, is that enough?" Zipping her jacket over the brightly colored shirt and pulling the hood over her dark curls, Serena almost disappeared. Faith looked down at her jeans, and red shirt. It wasn't black, but it was dark enough not to stand out. She glanced over at Claire and sighed. Her fluorescent green jogging suit was not ideal for sneaking around in the dark. If Jake looked out the window he may think aliens had landed.

"I haven't thought that far. Just be quiet, I don't want him to hear us." Faith pointed the light from her phone in front of them, leading the way.

They walked in silence except for the crunch of their shoes in the gravel. Every now and then a rustling from the tall grass hedging the roadside made Claire squeak and Faith hush her.

Finally nearing the house, they could make out a second vehicle parked next to Jake's truck.

"Son of a bitch!" Faith whispered a curse into the darkness.

"Wait, Faith." Serena, always the voice of reason, grabbed her arm in the darkness. "How do you know who it's for? It could be a brother or someone else."

"His brother's wouldn't be caught dead driving that yuppie-mobile." Faith glared at the vehicle.

"His mom?" Claire chimed in.

"His mother died years ago." Remembering the sweet lady that had always made her feel welcome, softened Faith's anger. Regret flooded through her. She hadn't been here when Jake's mother had been diagnosed or when she lost her battle with cancer.

"Sister?" Claire guessed again.

"He doesn't have any." Just lots of women friends Faith thought to herself.

"Don't jump to conclusions because of what some girl said. Find out for sure," Serena insisted.

"How?" Faith groaned frustrated. She needed to move and began to pace.

"Go knock on the door and ask him." Serena gracefully waved an arm toward the house.

"No. I can't." Faith shook her head miserably willing herself to breathe.

"I don't think we should slash the tires." Claire eyed the tires uncertainly. "We didn't bring a knife. Did you?"

"I was joking, Claire." Putting a hand to her head Faith began pacing again.

While trying to decide how she was going to get close enough to peek in the window, the front door opened. Jumping behind the truck before the shaft of light reached them, they squatted down to not be seen. Sneaking off into the azalea bushes that lined the driveway, Faith tried to get a better view. Faith pulled Claire with her hoping the green suit wasn't glowing in the porch light that had just clicked on. Muffled voices drifted closer to the doorway. One of them was definitely a female.

"I can't see," she heard Claire whisper through the rustling of branches.

"Shh." The voices were now on the porch.

"Jake, I don't know what you're so worried about. It's going to be great. You've never had performance anxiety before." Amy's voice was musical even when speaking.

Holding her breath, Faith watched through a small opening in the branches. The meatloaf special that had been sitting like a rock on her stomach since lunch began to roll.

Amy wrapped her arms around Jake and kissed him. Oh God. The meatloaf rock now rumbled. She felt sick. She couldn't tell who was kissing who, but it felt like an eternity too long to be the friendly hug of an acquaintance.

Amy finally let him go, picked up her guitar case and made her way to her car.

The friends stayed hidden as her car backed out the long drive way and disappeared. Not moving until the door closed and they were in darkness once more.

"Do you want to go talk to him?" Serena asked softly from somewhere in the hedges.

"What for? To be lied to. I'm done with that. Let's go." Faith pushed the branches out of her way, snapping a few in the process.

Walking slowly back down the driveway in silence, Faith lost all hope of ever being able to trust anyone again. Was this how it would be forever?

Half way back to the road, Claire's phone blasted out Fleetwood Mac into the darkness, startling them all.

"Oh, no!" Claire fumbled with her phone trying to turn it off.

The door to the house opened suddenly, and they could hear Jake's voice call out, "Hello?"

Faith grabbed Claire's hand and ran head first into the darkness. Somewhere near the end of the driveway, Faith lost her footing in a pothole and tumbled forward taking Claire with her. Serena, unable to stop, tripped over both of them. Scrambling to help each other off the ground, this time they didn't stop until they reached Claire's car. Huffing they climbed into the car and looked at each other. Faith, as mad as she was, couldn't stop herself from laughing. Serena's black suit was covered in dirt from her fall and her hair peeped out of the hood in wild tuffs. Claire had sticks and leaves stuck to her suit and hair. She reminded Faith of a mad fairy that had lost her wings. Knowing she looked just as rough, she didn't bother to look in the mirror.

"Does this mean Tequila?" Serena laughed as she tried to brush the dirt off of herself. The puffs of dust she created with each pat made them laugh harder. Faith was glad for the laughter. She knew if she couldn't laugh, she'd cry.

CHAPTER 18

"It's been days. Where is she?" Jake asked Gil impatiently walking up to the counter.

"She's around, man. I guess y'all just been missing each other," Gil shrugged. "You ain't been around much either."

"What are you talking about? I'm here every day." Jake's gaze swept the diner again, settling on the order window.

"But you don't eat." Gil sniffed sending him a sidelong glance. "You eating today?"

"Yeah, I guess so," Jake grumbled as he sat at the counter. "I've been busy. Getting ready to plant..."

He let the excuse die where it fell. He had been busy, but the music from the dream had been a constant distraction. Always pulling at him.

When he had left Faith that day, he had gone straight home to his guitar and the cheap keyboard he used to plink around on. The melody had come easily enough, but the words were more elusive. It wasn't the exact song from the dream, but the feelings were so intense. He had spent that entire day working it out in his head, afraid if he stopped it would be lost to him.

He had called Amy to get some feedback, someone to tell him he hadn't completely lost his mind. She had come willingly bringing food and her guitar, ready to work. To create. One thing they shared was their love of music. It had always been the common ground where their friendship grew and rooted, even through the awkwardness of finding out they weren't meant for each other.

By the time she left that night, they had the beginnings of a song. A song that made him happy, sad and relieved.

All of the jumbled up feelings he had no other way to express came out as music. He still couldn't remember the dream itself. It was more of a feeling, that feeling he couldn't shake after waking up. He remembered Faith crying and that house. That damn house. What was going on there? He was afraid for Faith, he didn't want her there. When he had finally stopped that night it was late. The diner had already closed. He had drove out to Serena's, thinking Faith might wait for him there. She wasn't there. So he had drove by her parents' house. Her car was there in the driveway. He didn't want to knock on the door and risk waking up her mom and dad, so he had called her. When she didn't answer, he assumed she was tired and had gone to bed. He went back home still thinking about the music. He had been so excited about what he and Amy had come up with. Amy suggested that once it was finished, they should record it. She wanted to help him get it out there for everyone to hear. He wasn't too sure about that. He just knew he had to finish it. So he had gone back home and worked on it some more. By morning he had another verse.

He knew Faith's kids were coming home on Sunday, so he had just left another message telling her to call whenever she could. By Monday, he had started to worry when he hadn't heard from her. He had driven by the diner, her house and even the old barn trying to catch her without her kids. Here it was the weekend again and she wasn't at work. He had lost count of the messages he had left on her voicemail. He knew he was starting to sound desperate and he didn't care.

He had the song finished and he really wanted her to hear it. To be the first to hear it since he had written it for her. The song he had sung at the bar, he had sang to her, but it had been someone else's words. He had tried to capture his feelings. All of the regrets and wasted time and finally the hope. The hope he felt for them and their future together. His future, all of his tomorrows, belonged to her. He didn't have anything to look forward to without her.

He finished his meal without tasting anything. It didn't matter, he couldn't think of anything but Faith. He was supposed to go out of town to meet Amy at the recording studio, but he hated to leave without seeing Faith first. He was tempted to wait for her at her dad's, but he had promised not to make things weird for the kids. He paid for his meal, grumbling when someone told him hello. He didn't bother looking up.

"What's with you? Girl troubles?" Gil teased. "Need some advice?"

"From you? I doubt it. I just got a lot on my mind."

"Whatever." Gil handed him his change, then added in a whisper, "Take my advice and come back for pie right before closing."

"Huh?" Suddenly he got it. "Umm... ok." Faith had been purposely avoiding him.

Walking back to his truck, he thought back to the last time he saw her standing on the porch of Serena's house. She had seemed fine. They had talked about the Coeur du Bayou sign. It had jumped out at him. He had chalked it up to being freaked out with everything else that had happened. It had all been unsettling, but familiar at the same time. From the feeling of being watched to telling her goodbye on the porch, it had been one huge Deja vu. He drove away wondering if she was hiding in the kitchen or out making a delivery.

Mulling it over as he drove the back roads, he realized he had driven straight to Serena's. That damn house. Faith wasn't there, but Serena's car was in the drive.

Maybe she could shed some light on what was going on. He went to the door and stood there, waiting to see if it would open for him like it had done before. Once again he was drawn to the sign. It seemed so familiar to him. The door stayed shut, so he knocked. It took a few moments but he could hear movement inside. Serena looked surprised for a few seconds, then smiled at him.

"Well, it certainly took you long enough."

"What?" Jake blinked at her in surprise.

"I figured you'd show up here eventually." She raised both eyebrows at him, "Looking for Faith?"

"Is she here?" Trying to peer around Serena, he shoved his hands in his pockets.

"No, she's not." Her dark curls bounced as she shook her head.

"That's ok." Jake shrugged, his gaze landing on the sign again. "I was hoping you could tell me why she's avoiding me."

"Is she?" Serena asked wide eyed.

"I think so. I went from seeing her every day to not seeing her for a week." He watched Serena's face as she thought for moment.

"Come in, Jake." She opened the door wider and he followed her inside to the parlor.

As he sat on the sofa, he took in the room. Not too frilly or formal, he relaxed a bit. "Nice room."

"Thank you." Serena sat across from him, placing her hands in her lap. "Now, why do you think she's avoiding you?"

"I don't know. She wanted to take it slow because of the kids, so I didn't worry the first couple of days." Running a hand through his hair, he sighed frustrated. "It's been a week and she hasn't returned any of my calls, not even a text. Is it because of the kids?"

"Honestly, hun, I can't answer that. I do know she's anxiously waiting for the divorce to be final and she has been very busy baking." Her simple reasoning was meant to calm him, but it didn't.

"Baking? Where?" His frustration growing, Jake's voice became louder echoing off the high ceiling.

She gave him a knowing smile.

"I've been by here at least twice a day and she's never here." Lowering his voice again, he pointed to the floor.

"She started parking in the back, to go straight in the kitchen." Serena looked down at her hands.

"Damn it. Her car is never at the diner either, and I know she's not parking in the back, because I've looked." He looked down at his boots miserably.

Serena's laugh filled the room. "Jake, did you ever figure out the dream with the music?"

"Why does that matter?" Jake asked uncomfortably, still looking at the floor.

"Because if it's the same music, it might have something to do with what's happening here. Happening to Faith." She leaned forward in her chair, drawing his attention.

"Did something else happen?" Immediately concerned, his head snapped up. He wondered to himself if another episode had caused her to stay away.

"No, she's been coming straight to the kitchen. Since most of the activity seems to happen in the foyer and upstairs. I was hoping that would help. So, I don't think she was hiding her car from you."

He just looked at her. She was so hard to read, he didn't have a clue if she was telling the truth or not.

"The music?" She prompted smiling at him again.

"I wrote a song. The song I dreamed about." It was out of his mouth before he realized it.

"Really?" She sat back considering.

"Yes, I went home that day and just had to get it out. I've been working on it since. My friend Amy came to help me. She wants me to record it." He put his head down. "I wanted to play it for Faith before I leave. It's for her."

Serena made a small noise, looking up he thought she was about to cry. "Oh, no."

"What?"

"Amy's the musician? She was helping you with the song. Of course," she added to herself.

"Yeah," Jake nodded his head in agreement, then stopped. "Wait. Of course what?"

"Nothing. Something just made more sense. You know, Jake, this song could mean something." She waved her hands in front of her, her face shining with excitement.

He eyed her suspiciously. "It does mean something. I wrote it for her. I guess it's a love song."

"Aren't they all?" Serena smiled at him knowingly.

He wasn't sure if it was the house, her or the combination of the two that made him so on edge. "Huh?"

"Songs. Every song is a love song. That's what they say." Serena shrugged.

"Oh yeah." Jake was so disturbed, her attempts to lighten the mood were lost on him.

"I meant that it could give us a clue as to what the presence is trying to tell us." She sat forward again, almost pleading.

"Like what? What could they tell us? They're dead. What would it matter?" Growing agitated again, he stood.

"Jake sit down, please," her voice concerned, she motioned to the sofa.

"Sorry, I just don't get it. I hate her being here. It scares me." He began to pace the room. She watched him closely for a moment considering his words.

"Are you scared to be here?" she asked quietly.

"No, not for me. Did you see her when that happened?" He turned to her, his tone on the verge of accusation.

"Are you uncomfortable here?" Ignoring his question, and his tone, she sat back crossing her legs.

"Yes, it's weird. This house..." he stopped, searching for the right words.

"What do you feel? Angry? Afraid?" she suggested.

"I don't know. Not angry exactly. It feels like something is not right. That morning, it felt like someone was watching me." The hairs on the back of his neck stood on end and a shiver ran down his back remembering the feeling.

"Really? Why didn't you say something?" Serena got up and crossed to a bookshelf.

"I don't know," he shrugged. "Does it really matter?"

"It might if you're connected to this too." Serena ran her hand over the side of a shelf, and he watched in awe as the bookcase opened.

"To what?" he asked as she disappeared behind it.

"To whatever they are trying to tell us or show us. Like when we found the sign that day. She led us to it. I think she wanted me to know." Serena reappeared flipping through the notebook he had seen her writing in the morning after Faith's dream. She returned to her chair and sat searching for the right page.

"Know what?" He wandered closer to the bookshelf and glanced curiously in the opening at a tastefully decorated office with a daybed in one corner.

"The house's name," she answered without looking at him.

"Coeur du Bayou," he whispered remembering his reaction to the sign that day. "That sign. I don't know if this means anything, but when I saw it that morning, I recognized it."

"Because you had seen it before when you were here?" Looking up from the book, she grabbed a pen from the side table.

"No, it was dark that night when she called me. I never noticed it." The hidden room forgotten, he paced as he recalled Faith's panicked call, and the terror he felt for her safety.

"So you saw it somewhere else?" Serena asked fishing for an explanation.

"No, I remembered it." He put a hand to his head agitated.

"Try to explain." Serena tapped the pen to the notebook.

"I was standing on the porch with Faith, telling her bye. I didn't want to leave her here. I saw the sign and it was like we had done this a thousand times before. I saw her there at the door, and the sign. It was like I was remembering something that never actually happened, but it felt like it did." Frustrated with his inability to explain, Jake began pacing again.

"Deja vu?" Serena stared off into space for a moment then began writing.

"Yeah, I guess." Jake suddenly tired, stopped pacing.

"Any other impressions?" she asked, still writing.

Jake sighing, shook his head. "I felt like I shouldn't be here, and I hated leaving her here."

He watched her scribble in the notebook not sure if anything in there would make a difference.

"So the song?" She smiled up at him. "That's exciting."

"Yeah, I'm supposed to leave tomorrow."

"Leave?" Putting the notebook on the table she looked at him in surprise.

"I have to go to the studio to record it. I'll be out of town for a few days. If I can't get in touch with Faith, will you tell her?" He knew he sounded pitiful, but at this point he needed to make sure Faith got the message.

"Of course." Serena stood, patting him on the arm.

"I've left messages. She doesn't call me back," he said miserably.

"I'm sorry. I think if you talk to her, this will all be straightened out. You'll see." Serena walked him into the foyer and opened the door.

"Ok, thanks." Seeing the open door, Jake had the urge to run through it. Walking quickly through the doorway instead, he stopped on the porch. "The diner should be closing. I'm going back over there."

Serena smiled at him, her eyes glittering. "Good idea."

CHAPTER 19

"We're going to need more pie," Gil called from the kitchen.

"That didn't last long," Faith laughed as she wiped down a table.

She smiled. If this kept up she'd really be able to bake full time. No more waitressing. She'd miss Gil and their lively conversations but she could visit when she delivered the desserts. He was doing his best to keep her laughing these last few days. She hadn't told him they went out to Jake's that night. He had guessed. She told him she didn't want to see Jake, so Gil said she could work in the kitchen when Jake came around.

Faith hated hiding in the back, but found it interesting that he kept coming around looking for her. The messages bothered her so much, after the first few, she hadn't listened to them. It still hurt and she hated it. She didn't remember it hurting this bad when David cheated on her. She knew she had to avoid Jake until she could get her emotions under control. She had trusted him and more importantly trusted her own feelings, only to be hurt again.

Moving to the next table, she began to clear the dishes. Spring was definitely here. The days had warmed considerably. She was hoping that as more green appeared her mood would improve, and by the time the flowers started blooming she would be happy again.

Her back was to the door when the bell jingled it's warning. Too late. She knew before she turned around that it was Jake. Turning slowly to look at him she willed herself to breathe.

"We're closed," she said without emotion trying to not look in his eyes.

"No, you're not." Pointing to the sign on the door, he gave her that lopsided grin. *Breathe.*

"Did you forget something?" Gil called innocently from the kitchen.

"Yeah, my pie," Jake said sarcastically rolling his eyes in Gil's direction.

"Have a seat," she snapped at Jake and sent a glare through the order window.

"Faith." Jake reached out to grab her arm as she made her way back to the counter.

"Don't touch me," Faith hissed at him sidestepping his reach.

"Whoa. Hey." He pulled back his hand. "What's wrong? I've been calling you all week. Why are you avoiding me?"

"Who said I'm avoiding you?" Safe behind the counter, she took a chance and looked into those chocolate eyes. *Breathe.*

"You haven't returned any of my calls and where were you when I came earlier?" He watched her closely his soft voice full of concern.

"I had work to do in the kitchen." Looking down at her shoes, she fidgeted with her apron. Her insides felt like jelly. She fought the urge to look at him.

"Yeah, right. What's going on Faith?" Jake sat at the counter, leaning forward on his crossed arms.

"What kind of pie do you want? I know you like pecan. Let me see what kind we have left." She strode briskly to the kitchen leaving the doors swinging wildly in her wake.

The bell from the door jingled again. Poking her head out of the order window, Faith saw Claire enter.

"Hey, I came a little early. Hope you don't mind," Claire called to her taking a seat at the counter.

"It's ok. I'll be done in a minute." Faith grabbed two pieces of pie not even looking at what kind they were. Remembering Claire's big mouth, she didn't want to leave Jake alone with her. Coming back through the doors, she noticed Claire was sitting at the counter wide eyed and red faced.

"Here's your pie," she said placing one of the plates in front of Jake, then giving the other to Claire. "I'll start cleaning up while you wait."

"Oh no. I don't need..." Claire tried to give the pie back.

"Go ahead and take it. I think I owe you," Jake said interrupting her.

Claire accepted the pie and muttered a small thank you.

"Are you going to tell me what's wrong?" He asked Faith again ignoring the pie in front of him.

"Absolutely nothing." Picking up the cleaner and rag, Faith gave him a fake smile over her shoulder.

Fleetwood Mac suddenly blared from Claire's pocket causing her to jump in mid bite. Putting down her fork she fished out her phone. She got up from her seat looking from Faith to Jake shyly. "It's Evan. I'll go outside." The door jingled as she said hello.

"That's it," Jake said pushing the pie away, his fork clattering in the aftermath.

"You don't want the pie?" Faith looked at the pie confused.

"Y'all were outside my house that night. You saw Amy leave." He gave her a sly smile. Proud that he had finally figured it out, he gave a two fingered drum roll on the counter.

"So you aren't gonna deny it?" Faith's free hand went immediately to her hip, her eyes flashing with anger.

"Of course not. I already told Serena." Jake shrugged easily.

"What?" Shocked, she put the cleaner and rag on the counter in front of her. A million things ran through her mind, and none of them were good. "Serena?"

"I just came from there. I told her what I've been trying to tell you but you won't answer my calls." He leaned forward again looking into her eyes. His warm brown eyes pleading with her.

The vision of Amy in his arms flashed before her in a red haze. "That Amy stays with you when she's in town."

"No, that she was helping me with the song." Jake shook his head as he explained.

"Hmmph....whatever."

"Faith..." His face a mixture of hurt and confusion. "I'm not lying. You haven't even listened to my messages, have you?"

"Jake, look. I'm a mess right now. I need to focus on my kids. I don't know what I was thinking. I'm too old to be playing games."

"I'm not playing games. I wrote a song. Amy helped me. I'm leaving tomorrow to go to the studio to record it." Jake stood, slapping his hands on the counter making the fork bounce again.

"That's nice Jake. I can put your pie in a to go container if you want to take it with you." Grabbing an empty container from the shelf behind her, she placed it on the counter next to his pie.

Dragging his hands over his face, he groaned in frustration. "Ok, Faith, there's obviously something else going on here and we're not going to get it cleared up tonight. I'm not going to fight with you."

"Well, that's a relief," she snorted grabbing her cleaning gear again to finish cleaning the tables. Claire came back in still blushing. Faith sent her a glare, as she rounded the counter.

"Evan always checks on me about this time." She blushed happily.

Jake looked at the time considering. "Yeah, he does. This is about the time y'all were creeping around in my yard."

"Ummm..." Claire looked at Faith unsure. "What?"

"I know y'all were there. I heard your phone." Jake motioned to the phone still in her hand.

"Oh, sorry." Claire grimaced realizing they were had. She tucked the phone back in her pocket.

"Are you here to take her home?" He nodded his head in Faith's direction.

"Yeah." Sitting back down, Claire watched them both uneasily.

"Take your pie to go. I've got it." He held out the container Faith left by his plate. Claire hesitated then took the container.

"No." Faith glared at them both, squirting the table down with dangerous intent.

"Faith we need to talk. I'll take you home." Jake took a few steps in her direction. *Breathe. Breathe.*

"I can walk. It's not that far." Turning her back to him again, she began wiping the table furiously.

"But your dad doesn't want you walking after dark," Claire blurted out, then looked down at her pie unsure of what to do.

Straightening back up Faith stood, and faced Jake. "Jake, I have a ride and there's nothing left to say."

"I'm not him." The simple statement shouldn't have had such an effect on her but the emotion in his voice broke her heart. Through blurry eyes she watched him throw money on the counter and walk out. The tears came out in a flood. Every tear she had forced herself not to cry all week finally broke free. She grabbed for a chair steadying herself.

"Faith, I'm so sorry. Sit down. I'll get some tissues." Claire jumped from the counter and pulled napkins from the dispenser.

"No. I've got to get this cleaned up." Unable to look at her friend, she wiped at the tears that fell onto the table.

Breathe. Breathe. Faith chanted still trying to fight back the tears unsuccessfully. She squeezed her eyes shut to block their path. Feeling a hand on hers, she opened her eyes as Gil gently took the rag out of her hand.

"It's ok. I'll finish up here. You let Claire take you home. I'm sorry. I thought if y'all would talk....." he shrugged his shoulders pitifully.

"No. It's not your fault," she whispered hoarsely.

Claire appeared holding her purse and jacket. "I've got your stuff. Let's get you home, or if you want you can come to my house."

"No, I just want to go home," Faith said without thinking. She honestly didn't know where that was.

"Come on. I'll lock up behind you. Don't worry about anything right now. Get some rest. Things will look better tomorrow," Gil was talking nervously as he walked them to the door.

"Yeah, sure." Faith said through her tears. The only thing she was sure about was that the only hope she had left for a happier future had just walked out that door with the jingling bell.

CHAPTER 20

"Mom, you sure you don't want to come?" Trent asked for the millionth time.

"Yeah, baby. I've got baking to do. You guys are going to have lots of fun. Bring your bags out to the car." Faith smiled at Trent and pulled on Hannah's dark ponytail as they passed through the kitchen carrying their backpacks.

David waited until the kids were out of the house before he put his arm around her. "What's wrong, babe?"

She pushed him away and leaned on the counter. Unphased he continued, "We missed you last weekend. You should come with us. I rented a cabin at this great place. It'll be fun."

Of course he wouldn't be out done with the camping trip. She should have known he'd be on the phone the next day renting a cabin to impress the kids.

"The kids are thrilled that you remembered. They'll love it." She tried to smile but the corners of her mouth just couldn't quite hold themselves up. Her face felt numb from crying half the night.

"Have you thought anymore about what I said?"

Faith should have known David wouldn't give up so easily. She was in no mood to be bullied.

"What did you say?" she asked picking up a coffee cup from the counter.

"About you coming home?"

Faith slammed the cup back down, turning on him. "I'm not coming back. Ever. Get that through your head. It's over."

His jaw clenched in anger.

"Oh, I'm sorry. For once you don't get your way. You'll just have to get over it."

"You're not yourself, Faith." David took a few steps back shaking his head. "Maybe it's hormonal."

"Hormones? You son of a bitch!" she screeched at him.

"Faith, calm down." His voice now raised to match hers.

"You lying piece of shit. Get out! You don't want me back, it would just look better to your friends. You use me like you use the kids, for your image." *Breathe. Breathe.*

"What are you talking about? You're not making any sense." His face reddened at her accusation.

"Of course I am. You want Trent home to play on the baseball team you sponsor. It looks bad that your son isn't there. That's it. Isn't it?" she laughed at him.

"No, I miss my kids, and to be honest I'm a little worried about them. All these stories about ghosts and you working at a diner." The disdain on his face was evident.

"Honest?" she snorted. "That's a laugh."

His face contorted into mask of anger as he opened his mouth. Before he could reply, the back door opened and Evan strode into the room glaring at David.

"I told the kids to wait outside. Faith, you ok?" Not taking his eyes off of David, Evan stood next to his sister.

"It's ok. He was just leaving. He's taking the kids camping." Faith glared at David daring him to say whatever he was thinking.

"Yeah, we better get going. Faith, I'll bring them back on Sunday. Evan, good to see you." David stalked out of the house, slamming the door behind him.

"Sis, you ok?" Evan finally turned to look at Faith.

"No." She poured a cup of coffee, handing it to Evan, then got another cup for herself.

"I'd beat him up for you, but the kids are here," he teased as he sat at the table.

"Speaking of..." Faith said as the back door opened again and her kids came racing in to say goodbye. After several hugs and kisses, she sent them back out the door and on to their adventure.

Once the door closed, Faith carried her cup to join her brother at the kitchen table. "I'm sorry."

"For hollering at that asshole? Don't be. I knew he was up to no good. I never liked that guy," he muttered into his coffee mug.

"I would have never guessed." Faith laughed rolling her eyes, then became serious again. "No, for the other day. Making Mom think Claire was pregnant. I shouldn't have done that."

"No, you shouldn't have. Mom was upset and you really embarrassed Claire." His tone was gruff, but his face showed no sign of anger.

"You really care about her, don't you?" Faith was amazed at the change in him, when it came to the subject of Claire.

"How did this become about me?" Evan almost choked on his coffee. "I came in here to keep you from killing that asshole. I heard you from outside."

"Did the kids hear?" She felt sick at the thought.

"I don't think so, they were at the car by the road. I was closer to the house. I didn't hear everything, just screaming and something about hormones. I figured I'd better interrupt before blood flowed." Evan grinned at her raising a dark brow. "His."

"Good. It just makes me so mad that he thinks he can bully me into going back." Faith gripped her cup and tried to calm herself.

"What? He's trying to make you go back. That son of a bitch." Evan sent a glare at the empty doorway.

"Don't worry. I think I made it clear." Faith laughed into her coffee.

"But will he take it out on the kids?" The worry on Evan's face was evident and warmed her heart.

"No, he won't. He's just not used to not getting his way." She took a sip of coffee then put her cup down thoughtfully. "Evan, why haven't you asked Claire to marry you?" she asked quietly.

"Faith...," he groaned.

"No really, I know you love her and she loves you. You have to know that."

"Yeah, I do." He looked down into his cup and sighed.

"So what are you waiting for?" Faith tried to imagine the reason he was dragging his feet, but came up with nothing.

"I just didn't think it was the right time." He shrugged without looking at her.

"Because?" she asked impatiently.

"Because you are in the middle of a divorce, and I don't ..."

"Evan Blaine," she whispered fiercely. "You haven't asked her because I'm getting a divorce?" Her voice was suddenly hoarse.

"Yeah, it just didn't seem right." He shrugged his shoulders again this time watching her with concern.

"That's so sweet." She wiped at her eyes. The last thing she needed was to turn on the water works again.

"It's just you were finally starting to be ok, or I thought you were." Evan gestured with his hands trying to explain his reasoning. "I didn't want to upset you again, or the kids. I don't know. It sounds stupid now, but it just didn't seem right."

Her heart felt like it was being squeezed. *Breathe. Breathe.* "Two weeks?"

"What?" He gave her a confused look.

"My divorce is final in two weeks. So you'll ask her then?" Faith's hand gripped her brothers arm squeezing.

"Well, I don't know. I haven't set a time." A look of panic crossed his face.

"Evan, do me a huge favor?" Pulling on his arm again, she gave him a huge grin.

"What?" he asked suspiciously.

"Walk your ass across the yard and ask her to marry you. Please. Nothing would make me happier right now than knowing that two of my favorite people are happy. The kids will be excited, too. They love Claire. We all do." Tugging on his arm she almost came out of her chair with excitement.

"I'd love to, Sis, but I'm not fully prepared. Got to get the ring, and I'm thinking I'll bring her out somewhere, don't you think?" Serious again, a dark strand of hair fell over his forehead as he leaned forward.

"He's smarter than he looks, folks." She smiled at him punching him on the arm. "Just don't wait too long."

"I'm going to town later." Evan frowned at her. "Gotta buy a tent. I'll look around then."

"Yes, the party. I need to start making plans for that," Faith groaned rubbing her forehead. *Breathe.*

"So the asshole's taking them camping? Does that mean we don't have to invite him?" Sitting there with his large hands wrapped around his mug, Faith noticed again the striking resemblance to her father.

"No, as much as I'd love to see him sleeping on the cold ground, I don't think it would be a good idea."

"Just not too many kids, ok? I don't want to have to buy a circus tent." The wooden chair creaked as Evan pulled himself up from the table.

"I'm sorry. I thought you'd already have one." Still cradling her head she rubbed at her temples.

"For what?"

"I don't know. It's a guy thing." Faith shrugged rolling her eyes.

"My sleeping on the ground days were over long ago, but for Trent I'll make the sacrifice. You'll owe me." He tugged playfully at her ponytail.

"You'll have kids one day. I'll make every last one of their birthday cakes," she teased waiting for him to freak out, but he just smiled down at her.

"Yes, you will, little sister." His dark eyes gazed out the kitchen window for a moment, then he turned and leaned against the counter. "So enough about me, what about you and Jake? How's that going?"

"It's not," Faith answered without thinking, the sadness pulling at her.

"What happened?" Pushing away from the worn counter Evan stood straight, suddenly tense.

"Nothing. Just taking it slow. The kids, the divorce..." she sipped her coffee trying to act casual.

Evan nodded with understanding. "Claire said you had another ghost thing."

"Yeah, it was so weird, but nothing's happened since then. Maybe it's over." She shrugged her shoulders, hoping it was true.

"It is weird. I don't know why you even go over there." Relaxing again he leaned back on the counter.

"To bake. In fact, I guess I'd better get over there." Glancing at the faded rooster on the clock, she sighed. "We're out of pie at the diner."

"You know, you could bake one for your loving brother." Faith just rolled her eyes at him as she got up to rinse out her cup.

"Where's Mom and Dad?" he asked then drained the rest of his coffee.

"They said they had to go into town but I think they just didn't want to be here when David got here."

"Probably for the best, Mom would be washing your mouth out with soap right about now." Evan grinned and handed his cup to her. They both laughed. Annoying as he could be at times, she wouldn't trade him for anything. She smiled as she thought about his wedding. A glimmer of hope shone through her sadness.

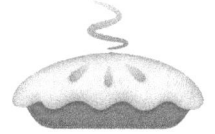

CHAPTER 21

"Take a break." Mac shook his shaggy head at them through the glass, his gravelly voice coming through the speaker into the booth.

"No, I'm good." Jake rubbed a clammy hand over his jeans again. He was still sweating but not nearly as bad as the first day.

Mac gave him that sour look that had often crossed his face over the past few days. "Yeah, man. Whatever. I gotta piss. Take a break anyway."

As Mac rose from his chair, Jake couldn't help picturing him dressed in worn battle armor, dragging a bloodstained war hammer behind him as he trudged dutifully off to the pisser. The recording engineer's dirty blonde hair and beard combined with his short stature reminded Jake of a dwarf of Middle Earth. His gruff nature completed the package. Looks aside, he was all wizard when it came to sound.

"No, you're exhausted and I think we both need to step away for a while," Amy said pointedly tugging off her headphones.

"I need this done." Watching her unstrap her guitar, Jake knew there was no arguing.

"Yeah, I know, but you're the one who changed everything." Putting her guitar on a stand, she glanced over her shoulder at him. Taking in her rumpled appearance, he knew he looked worse.

"Sorry, I had to." Jake had left the diner that night so hurt and pissed off, he had gone home, tore the song apart, rearranged it and changed the words. Now it was real and complete. Those feelings were now a living thing that everyone would hear. He hoped it conveyed the depth of emotions he had felt while writing it out.

Getting it recorded just seemed to be taking an extremely long time. Not very familiar with the recording process, this marathon session in the studio had given him a new appreciation for those who seemed to have a knack for it.

"Coffee?" Amy asked as he followed her into the break room.

"No. I think my nerves are jangled enough. Just water and some air." Looking around the windowless room he pulled at the neck of his shirt uncomfortably.

"Sounds good. Need company?"

"Sure." Grabbing bottles of water, they headed out into the sunlight.

The studio not having any windows was an obstacle he had never considered. The first day there had been horrible, with many breaks and lots of sweating. There were several times he wanted to call it quits, but Amy had talked him through it. This song was important to him. He needed to finish it and he needed for Faith to hear it. Amy's laughter broke through his thoughts making him smile into the sun. "What?"

"You're like a dog I had once." Amy grinned at him through the curtain of her dark hair, one dimple showing on her ivory skin.

"What do you mean? I'm cute and furry?" he asked scratching the stubble on his chin. The days had bled together. With their scheduled time nearing an end, Mac had offered to fit them in around other artists so they could finish.

"Just the way you're standing there with your face to the sun. Eyes half open. I'm waiting for you to start panting." She giggled, the dimple becoming more pronounced.

"I just might." Jake breathed in deeply, loving the fresh air and warm sun on his skin.

"Have you always been so claustrophobic?" In the sunlight, streaks of red flamed through her hair, and Jake found himself wondering if she ever wore her hair in a ponytail. Faith's face immediately came to mind, her eyes flashing with heat and passion. Memories of the old barn, and her tanned skin in the sun hovered before him. He shook his head to dispel the thoughts, but they were never completely gone.

"I don't know. I've never noticed because I'm always outside. I had no idea." He had to chuckle at himself.

"It's good to hear to you laugh." Twisting the bottle open, Amy took a sip of water.

"It feels good, too." He nodded his head in agreement, turning his face back towards the sun.

"You know Jake," she said leaning against the side of the building, "This song is great, even though it hurts, everybody is going to love it. That's the irony of it."

"Yeah, well, just between me and you, I'm not sure I can handle too many more broken hearted songs." The hurt was there too, never gone, just a dull ache in his heart. Some if it he had been carrying around for a long time. Faith had to listen to the song. There had to be a way to fix this.

"Well, if you ask me, I think you need to finish this song. Then go back home and let her hear it. Then get married, make lots of babies and sit on your porch writing happy songs." The water in her bottle sloshed around as she swung her hand back and forth as she talked.

"That sounds like an awesome plan." He turned from the sun to give her his lopsided grin, his brown eyes twinkling. "That, I know I could do and die a happy man doing it."

"Oh wow," Amy said slowly, her eyes suddenly huge. She pushed herself off of the wall, her face unreadable.

"What?" Jake was hoping she wasn't ready to drag him back inside just yet. His mouth became dry at the thought of the windowless room.

"You just gave me an idea. Take your time. I've got to write this down." Jake watched her through half open eyes as she practically ran back into the studio. Rolling his shoulders and stretching his back, he thought of Amy's dog. He laughed at himself, glad she hadn't been there to see that.

He had known he wasn't cut out for life on the road. The traveling required of professional musicians would be torture for him. Now he knew studio work was not his cup of tea either. Amy had the right idea. He could still play music every now and then, writing songs when he felt like it. He would be happy with that. The picture she had painted in his head included Faith on his porch, her kids playing in the yard, and by God he had even seen a baby on his lap sleeping peacefully. Where had that come from? He didn't know, but the picture was a nice one. Smiling into the sun again, he could picture how perfect it would be and it gave him hope.

CHAPTER 22

"Why didn't you tell me?" Evan's gruff voice from behind her made Faith jump.

"Tell you about what?" Thankful she had already fixed the campfire on the cake, or it could have ended in a forest fire disaster. Faith turned and glared at him.

"About Jake."

Faith gave her brother a guilty look, afraid to say anything.

"Recording a song? That's a big deal. I had to hear it from Helen. The whole town's talking about it." He looked at her perplexed.

"Oh....are they?" Faith pretended to study the cake in front of her.

"Yeah, come on. You knew right?" He eyed her suspiciously leaning on the counter.

"Of course. He told me before he left." It wasn't a lie, Jake had told her. She just hadn't believed him.

"Then why don't you seem happy about it?" Her brothers dark eyes had narrowed on her, making her more uncomfortable.

"Happy?" Faith turned her attention back to the cake.

"Happy for him?" Evan needled.

Reaching for an icing bag, she tried changing the subject. "Look, I really need to get this cake finished before everyone gets here. Are you ready for tonight?"

"Yeah, I'm going to set up the tent back there." Standing up straight Evan motioned to the area behind the house.

"Ok, great." Glad to be off the subject of Jake, she searched through the icing tips for the one she needed for grass.

Evan started to leave the kitchen, then turned back to his sister, "Did something else happen?"

"Huh?...." Faith turned back to him surprised, "Oh, ghost wise? No, I've been so busy, if they're trying to get my attention, I haven't noticed."

"Ok." Nodding his head he took a minute to examine her work on the cake. A stand of trees lined the back edge of the cake and a small yellow tent stood erect next to a tiny campfire with orange and red flames surrounded by miniature rocks. "That's cool, Sis. Has Trent seen it yet?"

"Not yet." She smiled as she stepped back to admire her own work.

"He's going to love it. My tent is not yellow though," he teased still admiring the cake.

"I don't think he'll care. I've got stuff for the s'mores and chips for them to snack on later, if they get hungry." Faith pointed to a grocery bag on the counter behind her.

"Sounds good and sticky." Evan laughed then became serious again. "Was asshole still butt hurt that he wasn't invited?"

A giggle escaped before she could answer. "No, I think he was impressed with himself over their camping trip, but I know having them two weekends in a row must have put a cramp in his social life."

"So he's leaving you alone?" Apparently her brother's Spidey senses were tingling, and he was trying hard to find out what was wrong with her.

"Yeah, I was pretty clear and I'm waiting on the papers any day now. Maybe the lawyer will call," she shrugged indifferently. She had once thought those magical papers would restore her hope and somehow bring her happiness. She knew better now.

"Hello?" Claire's cheerful voice called from the front door.

"In the kitchen," Faith answered her hoping the interruption would distract Evan.

"Hey, Darlin'." Evan greeted Claire by wrapping his arms around her with a kiss so steamy it almost made Faith blush.

Faith cleared her throat loudly, "I'm still in the room. I'd tell y'all to get a room, but Brother Dear has work to do."

A blushing Claire reluctantly pulled away from Evan, her big blue eyes twinkling with excitement. "Where's Serena?"

"I don't know. Baton Rouge or New Orleans. Something about Zumba. She doesn't want to do it, so I don't know why she went." Faith's ponytail bobbed as she shook her head with worry, turning back to her search through the metal tips.

"Oh, when is she coming back?" The disappointment in Claire's voice made Faith turn back to Claire.

"I don't know. Why?"

"I wanted to tell y'all at the same time." Her face glowed with happiness as Claire held out her left hand and squealed, "We're getting married!"

The shimmering princess cut diamond sat prettily on entwining bands of white gold and smaller diamonds, prompting a gasp of appreciation from Faith.

"Yes!" Faith hugged Claire first, then her brother adding, "I knew you could do it."

"I didn't need you to bully me." Evan hugged her back

"Me, bully? Never." Faith rolled her eyes as the tears began to gather.

"Hey." Evan pulled on her ponytail as she turned away. "You, ok?"

"Yeah." Faith wiped at her eyes. "Happy tears. Tears of relief that my brother isn't really all that slow."

"Yeah, whatever." Evan ignoring his sister's jab turned his attention back to Claire. "I'll get started on the tent, if my lovely assistant is willing to help." He held out a hand to her.

In that moment, Faith wished she had a camera to capture the looks on both of their faces. She sighed inwardly. She knew Claire was dying to give her the details. Evan had been so secretive about the whole thing, of course. Wondering if she was the first to know she asked out loud, "Hey, does Mom know?"

"Not yet. We thought we'd wait till they got here, but I had to tell you. I couldn't wait." Claire beamed at her. "Should we wait until after the party?"

"Just until the cake is cut. The kids will be scattered out in the yard after that. We don't want Mom scaring them." Faith laughed then added in an ominous voice, "There will be tears."

"I know. After that baby incident...." Evan grimaced remembering. "Hey, we can have a party later. Celebrate our engagement and your divorce. I know Jake will be happy about that."

The mention of Jake's name had her stomach fluttering. "Oh, yeah.... No, I mean, it should be about y'all. I've got the cake covered."

"What if I want pie?"

"No," Claire answered for her, "We want cake. A beautiful cake."

"We're not even married yet, and she's already telling me what I want," Evan teased, pulling Claire close and kissing her on the forehead. "Come on. We've got a tent to set up."

"Ok, I'll be there in a minute." Claire gazed up at him shyly.

He looked from Claire to his sister suspiciously, "What are y'all up to?"

"Nothing. I just want to talk to her. Girl stuff." Claire smiled at him patting him on the chest.

"Yuck." He made a face then smiled at Claire, "I'll be out back." They watched him leave the room and waited until they heard the heavy front door close.

"You told him to ask me?" Face still flushed and rosy, Claire gazed dreamily at her ring.

"No, I told him to not wait." Faith admired the glittering ring again. "And he picked that out on his own."

"Really?"

"Yes." Faith felt her eyes water again. "Claire, I'm so happy for you."

"Me, too." Claire grinned, then frowned, "What about Jake?"

"What about him?" Faith turned back to the cake not happy with the direction of the conversation.

"Everyone in town is talking about him." Claire rounded the counter island to look at Faith across the unfinished cake.

"So?" Finally finding the tip she had been searching for, she put it on the bag screwing the coupler together.

"Faith, I think he was telling you the truth about the song." Claire watched as Faith loaded the bag with green icing.

"You been talking to Serena?" Serena had been certain it was the truth. Maybe it was. They wrote a song. It didn't mean there wasn't anything else going on.

"No, she hasn't been around much."

"You've noticed that too? I'm kinda worried about her." Faith looked up at her as she twisted the end of the bag, then put it down.

"Is she that upset over the Zumba thing?" Claire asked concerned.

"No, she said she wasn't going to do it. They could get another instructor, and she could still do belly dancing for those that wanted to keep doing it." The icing bag forgotten again, Faith bit her lip worried about Serena. "I think the ghost stuff is bothering her more. She thought she'd be open by now. I've been so wrapped up in my own problems, and you know how she is. More concerned about what's going on with everybody else."

"Yeah, you're right." Putting her hands on the counter, Claire leaned forward. "When she gets back we need to get together, and help her finish that room. It'll be fun."

Faith smiled at Claire. Not only had she been a good friend, she would now officially be family. Grinning she grabbed Claire's hand to look at the ring again.

"Oh my God! We get to plan a wedding!" she squealed with excitement.

Claire beamed as she gazed down at the ring. "You know what else this means, right?"

"I'm making the cake. I'll be your maid of honor, and godmother to all of your children?" Faith asked matter-of-factly.

Claire giggled, then shook her head, "No, you're next!"

CHAPTER 23

The party was a huge success, her part of it anyway. The food, the cake and the presents were done. Evan was in charge of the actual sleep in the tent portion of the evening. She grinned thanking God she didn't have to do that.

As she picked up the trash and half empty punch cups from the porch, she could hear the wild whooping of Trent and his friends from the woods. They had marked the trail again with the solar lights in case any of them needed to come back to the house during the night. She'd sleep in the parlor to be nearby if anyone needed her. She didn't mind, the sofa was more comfortable than the ground. After the cleanup, she planned to do some baking to keep herself busy.

The exciting news of Evan and Claire's engagement had sent Margaret into a flurry of happy tears and rushed plans for the wedding.

Evan had to step in and remind everyone that a date had not been set, which of course, led to the immediate discussion of the best time to get married. By the time their parents had left, Evan was glad to march off into the woods with the boys. Her father, who seemed excited by the news also, would probably be sick of hearing about it by the end of their drive home. Hannah's pouting threatened to suck the joy out of Trent's party, so Claire had offered to have a sleepover with her and the soon to be mom, Rosie.

Faith was thrilled, and already thinking of cake designs and colors to suggest to the bride to be. This wedding gave her hope. Maybe that's why she enjoyed making cakes so much. Sure, she loved the creative part of it, but there was more to it than that. Celebrations, weddings, babies, and even birthdays, were all new beginnings. New beginnings filled with promise and hope.

Back in the kitchen, she washed the trays and put them away. Then getting the ingredients ready, she went to work on a pie. She wondered when Serena would be home. Faith hoped she wouldn't be too upset that she had missed the big announcement. She seemed to be gone quite a bit recently. Faith wasn't sure if it had to do with the exercise classes or if it was because of the house stuff. She knew the delay in opening had to be taking a toll on her, but she got the feeling that it had more to do with the ghostly happenings than money issues. Ever since they had become friends,

Faith had wondered how she was able to afford the renovations, but assumed it was a loan. Serena had never sweated over the opening date coming or going, so Faith had never asked about it. Remembering her and Claire's plan to help with the room upstairs, she thought about the way the room had looked in her vision. As always the measuring, mixing, and rolling out of the crust, calmed her.

She had given Serena all the details she could remember. The light yellow of the walls had been comforting. The sparseness of the furnishings had felt freeing, not like the cumbersome heavy modern furniture. Maybe the ghost lady just wanted her room the way it had been. Could it be that simple?

With the pies in the oven, she cleaned up the new mess, grateful to not have another cake to make for at least a week. Her back was starting to ache, that usually meant it was time to rest. She put the tea kettle on, and as the timer ticked away she thought about Jake.

She had tried to put him out of her mind all week, but everyone kept bringing him up, except for Gil, who went out of his way not to mention him. She guessed he was still feeling guilty about what happened even though it had nothing to do with him. Evan, on the other hand, with his sudden change of heart had her afraid to mention anything about Amy. With all of the talk about Jake and his song, no one had ever mentioned his relationship with Amy. Tracey was the only one to bring it up. Maybe Helen, Gil, Serena and everyone else was right.

She recalled the look on his face that day when he realized she hadn't listened to the messages. It was a mixture of disbelief and hurt.

Finally the timer dinged, and she took the pies out to cool. Pouring hot water over the teabag, she decided it was time to listen to his messages. Maybe she was letting her own bad marriage and trust issues cloud her judgement. Bringing her tea and her phone into the parlor, she sat and dialed her voicemail. Twenty four messages. She knew he had called more than that. He had probably started hanging up instead of leaving messages. She didn't blame him. The first few were just 'hey call me', then she could hear the concern growing with each call. Her tea forgotten she continued to listen. Message after message, concern, hurt and finally desperation. By the time she was done clearing all the messages, she was in tears. It was obvious he cared. Even in David's best plea for forgiveness, there had not been so much concern and love for her.

Wiping her eyes, she thought about calling him. It was late and she really didn't know what to say. 'Start with I'm sorry,' she snorted to herself.

Walking to the door, Faith decided to get some air and see if she could still hear the boys. She figured by now they were either telling ghost stories or fast asleep. She pulled on the heavy door, surprised when sunlight blinded her.

"Oh!" she gasped putting a hand over her eyes to peer through the light.

"I'm sorry. I didn't mean to frighten you." A deep voice seemed to come from within the light startling her more. The hand that had been over her eyes moved to cover her mouth. She struggled to focus her eyes on the man that stood before her. Her laboring vision slowly revealed a handsome young man in tidy antique work clothes. His clean shaven face was friendly and a playful grin teased the edges of his mouth.

"The sign your father ordered." The voice sounded familiar and made her smile. The young man held out the sign to her. It was the Coeur du Bayou sign they had found in the upstairs closet, but freshly carved and painted.

"It's beautiful!" she heard herself say, but it wasn't her voice. What was going on?

"Not as beautiful as you, Mademoiselle," he leaned in to whisper conspiratorially, smiling at her with a familiar lopsided grin. She reached out a hand to touch his face. She knew this man. The faint scent of gardenias enveloped her.

Suddenly, no longer on the porch, she found herself entwined passionately with this man. The smell of hay and horses surrounding her. She loved this man dearly, the feeling consumed her. Trying to recall his name she felt it on her lips, but his murmurings of love and forever filled her so completely she was lost.

She cried out in frustration. The pain was blinding. Through the haze of it she heard her own screams as if from a far off place. No longer in the barn, her eyes searched the dimly lit room for her lover, but he was not there. She knew he wasn't and he would never be again. The only thing left of him was the babe she was laboring so hard to bring into this world she no longer wanted to live in.

Faith found herself on the porch shivering. The phantom pains of childbirth burned into her memory and the sadness in her heart lingered like a bad dream.

Wishing she had a name for the man, her lover, she searched through her memory to recall it. It seemed important somehow. Maybe the ghost was trying to find him. He had made the sign, and she had loved him, of that much Faith was certain. The sign had been hidden away for a long time. There must have been a reason.

Faith went inside in search of paper and pen to write everything down she could remember. Thinking of the baby made her sad. Holding her stomach, she remembered the pain. That room had been different and not at all familiar to her. She struggled to remember the faces of the people that were with her. It had been dark, and they had seemed to be in the shadows. She could still feel the humid air and her sweat soaked gown. Through the pain she had not been able to focus on their faces, but the voices had been comforting. She wrote down as much detail as she could remember, however the unbearable sadness she had felt was hard to describe in words.

As her hands gripped at her flat stomach, she was reminded of the earlier encounter in the upstairs room, crying for her baby. If there had been a baby, which from the memories she was pretty sure there had been, what had happened to it? Had it died? The awful sadness returned. How awful to lose a baby after losing her lover. No wonder she cries. Faith had only gotten a glimpse of her pain, she couldn't imagine having to live with it forever.

Wrapping herself in a throw she curled up on the sofa and cried herself into a dreamless sleep.

CHAPTER 24

"Are you sure about this color?" Serena asked rolling the pale yellow paint onto the wall.

"Yes, it's as close as I can remember. Don't you like it?" Sitting on the floor, Faith carefully painted around the masking tape admiring the sunny color.

Making good on their promise to help Serena finish the room, Claire and Faith had surprised her with the paint, declaring it a work day.

"I love it. I'm hoping the ghost woman likes it too. So far so good." Serena's dark eyes wandered around the room. "She's been quiet."

"Can you feel her?" Claire whispered loudly over the faint sound of the radio and the squishing noises from the roller.

"No, it's calm." Serena paused pushing a curl off her forehead. Small yellow specks of paint colored her tanned hands and blue work shirt.

"So you think this will work and she'll stop?" Faith felt the sadness pulling at her again. Her thoughts had been torn between Jake and the grieving ghost. The only bright spot since the wedding announcement had been her kids' anticipation for Easter, but even that had made Faith sad. Her kids would be spending Easter with David and his family.

"I don't know. I really don't think it's about the room. She wanted us to find the sign. It meant something to her and now we know why." Serena smiled sadly at Faith then continued rolling the paint.

"I wish I knew his name or hers even. You didn't get any names off the graves out there?" Faith asked remembering the heat of their passion in the barn. Immediately Jake and their secret meetings came to mind. Keeping her head down, she willed herself to not start crying again.

"I tried making imprints, but even with the rubbings the stones were so decayed. It's hard to make out any of the letters or dates."

"And there wasn't a baby's grave?" It disturbed Faith that the baby wasn't there.

"No, but the tomb could hold several bodies," Serena pointed out.

"Do you think it's over?" Working on her spot on the opposite wall, Claire had stripes of yellow paint trailing down her side where the paint had dripped from her brush.

"What do you mean?" The roller squeaked as Serena pushed it up and down the wall.

"Do you think that she'll stop crying? We found the sign and now we know why," Claire said without turning from her spot.

"I don't know. We're painting. Usually by now there's door slamming." Serena pushed her roller through the paint pan again.

"Do you think you'll open soon?" The excitement in Claire's voice had Faith suspicious.

"Why?" Faith narrowed her eyes at Claire's back. "What's going on Claire?"

"Evan and I have been talking about the wedding." Turning from the wall, Claire's grin was huge. "We'd like to get married here."

"Yes!" Faith jumped up from the floor, brush still in hand. "Did y'all set a date?"

"No, not yet. That depends on Serena, and when she'll be ready to open." Claire said pointing her brush at Serena. A giant blob of paint plopped onto the drop cloth.

"Oh, no, you don't. Don't hang that on me. If you wanted to get married tomorrow, I'd be setting out chairs down stairs or out on the lawn...." Serena's eyes glazed over and her voice drifted off.

"Serena? Are you ok?" Claire's blue eyes were huge with concern.

Serena stared blankly towards the window. "Oh, yes," she whispered. Finally her gaze found Faith. "Weddings...events. I'm so stupid. I was so focused on renting out the bedrooms that I totally missed the fact that I could be hosting events here." She put the roller back into the pan slowly. "I have the big room downstairs. I can add tables or chairs. Faith, you can cater the food."

Faith dropped her paint brush sending droplets of yellow paint across the plastic covered floor. *Breathe. Breathe.* Putting a hand to her heart, her mouth moved but no sound would come out.

"Faith? It's a good idea, right?" Claire asked nervously crossing the room to her friends.

Still unable to speak, Faith simply nodded her head in agreement.

"Oh Claire, it's the best idea ever and your wedding will be the first, I promise." Serena hugged Claire carefully avoiding the loaded brush she was still holding. "Oh this is great! This is so exciting. Faith?" She turned to Faith, who still hadn't moved.

"I need to sit or something." *Breathe. Breathe.* Faith took a deep breath and sat back down on the floor putting her head between her knees.

"Is something happening?" Kneeling down next to Faith, Serena picked up the forgotten brush and put it in the tray.

"No," Faith looked up slowly at her friends her eyes shining, "It's like everything is finally starting to make sense again. I think I can breathe. We can do this. I know it."

"Of course we can." Serena patted her on the shoulder.

"What about you? Can you do this?" Faith asked desperately.

"I had already decided against the Zumba thing. I had planned to offer to keep the belly dancing class going for those of you that want it, but I can work around that. If scheduling is our only problem..." She shrugged indifferently sitting next to Faith, "We can belly dance here."

"Holy smokes, Batman. This could work." Faith giggled picking up her brush again and pointing it at Claire. "So, Claire, you set a date and let's get this going. Don't let my slow ass brother drag his feet."

"Oh, this is a dream come true." Claire smiled down at them hugging herself, another blob of paint dripped on her shirt. "Actually, it is... Serena's dream."

"Yes, it is, in a way." Serena's smile was halfhearted as she gave Faith a sideways glance. Faith knew Claire was referring to them all getting married. She shook her head dipping her brush in the paint. Faith was excited for Claire and Evan, but the ink on her divorce papers was still as slick as the paint on her brush.

"That reminds me. I have something for you. I'll be right back," Claire started then turned to put her brush down.

"Don't step in the paint," Serena cautioned her.

"Ok." Stepping carefully around the paint splatters, Claire made her way out of the room.

Faith and Serena could hear Claire moving around downstairs. Faith thought about the ghost lady and the love that was denied her. Once again, Jake came to mind and the similarities made her uncomfortable. When Claire came bounding back up the stairs, Faith was glad to have her thoughts interrupted.

Claire caught herself before rushing into the room. Stepping gingerly around the paint spills, she held out a small wooden sign to Serena. "I saw this when we were paint shopping. It reminded me of you and this room. I thought it would look nice in here."

The light blue background on the hand painted sign instantly brought back soft memories of Trent as a baby. Faith was reminded of the smell of baby powder and the sweet feeling of rocking a sleeping baby. The whimsical lettering of bright yellow spelled out "Bon Reve". The friends gasped all at once as the smell of gardenias washed over them overpowering the smell of the fresh paint.

"I love it!" Serena smiled at Claire. "I think she likes it too."

"It means sweet dreams," Claire announced proudly looking around the room.

"It's perfect." Hugging the sign to her chest, Serena struggled to her feet to hug Claire again.

"Oh...oh. Oh." Claire pushed out of Serena's arms and ran to the radio in the corner of the room. "It's our song!"

As she turned the volume up the familiar song floated through air.

"Don't stop thinking about tomorrow... It'll soon be here."

CHAPTER 25

Jake had been away from home too long. The claustrophobic feeling from the studio was enough of an obstacle, but he was homesick, too. He needed to get back to the familiar landscape of the fields, the friendly faces of Cypress Point and, of course, Faith. He hadn't heard from her since the day at the diner. He still hoped she would call after listening to the messages. Maybe she deleted them without listening to them. He still wasn't sure what had happened.

He'd deal with that once he got home, if he ever got there. Recording the song had taken longer than he expected. Mac worked them in at odd times over the week, to finish up. With the constant breaks for Jake's anxiety and Mac's perfectionism, it had been torture. If the song wasn't so important to him, he'd have been back in Cypress Point after the first day of recording. It was important. He needed for those feelings to be expressed and he needed for Faith to hear it. He knew without a doubt once Faith heard the song, she would understand everything. She had to.

When Mac finally gave his blessing on the final cut, Amy decided they should do a whirlwind tour of local radio stations to promote the song and get air play. Not understanding the importance of the publicity, Jake just followed along, answering questions and before he knew it another week had passed. Now he was trying to get home for Easter and he was going to make it. Driving like a madman, the closer he got to Cypress Point the faster he drove.

He did have to admit he felt a rush the first time his song came over his truck radio unexpectedly. Amy had called and left him a message, something about people buying it and downloading. It was a bit overwhelming. Now, if Faith would only listen to it. Jake had wanted to sing it to her in person before he left. He knew it would have meant so much more, but her and her ponytail were being pigheaded.

The blinking of the gas light caught his attention, and he groaned in frustration looking for a roadside sign to indicate how far he was from home. If he was lucky, he would make it to the station just outside of Cypress

Point. Driving the last few miles, he began to relax. His thoughts returned to Faith, and the years that had passed. He thought of the photo albums in the trunk of her car. He wanted that. He wanted pictures of them together happy and he'd make damn sure it showed in her eyes.

Rolling up to the pumps, Jake sighed with relief. His sigh turned into a groan when he noticed Tracey McMillian waving at him from across the gas station parking lot. Before he could open his door, she was running to him. Well, not actually running, in those tight jeans and heels it looked more like an awkward shuffle.

Again the contrasts between her and Faith were startling. Faith wore her jeans tight, but they molded around her curves comfortably. Tracey looked like she had been stuffed into a pair that were three sizes too small. Her painted face was attractive, but he knew if she scrubbed it off, the difference in her appearance would be disturbing. Faith on the other hand barely wore any make up. Some people might call her plain looking, but her natural beauty and simple ponytail drove him crazy.

Tracey obviously thinking the smile on his face was for her locked him in a forceful hug that nearly toppled them both. "Oh, Jake, honey! I'm so excited for you. Your song is awesome!"

"Thanks." Jake pulled away from her putting distance between them and taking a step back for good measure.

"Everyone just loves it. The whole town has been talking nonstop about you." Her shiny red nails reached for him again. Pretending he didn't notice, he reached for the cap on his gas tank.

"That's great, Tracey." He smiled at her as he filled his tank. "Hey, do you know if Faith is working at the diner today?"

"No, I haven't seen her around much lately. They've been busy down at the old Amie' place." Smiling back at him, she pushed out her chest.

"Oh? Serena's finally opening?" Trying to not encourage her, he watched the numbers flipping on the pump.

"No, the wedding, silly. It's the second biggest news in town. The Bertrand wedding at the haunted house. I guess since Faith is friends with that weird girl, she's letting them get married there. I knew they'd get back together. She was stupid to let him go." Glancing over her shoulder, as if she cared if someone would hear her, Tracey turned back to Jake with a smile. "I've got to run. See ya' around and congrats again."

Shuffling her way back to her car, Jake stood watching mouth open, gas nozzle in hand. There's no way. Faith wouldn't take him back. Numbly putting the nozzle back on the pump, he forced himself to breathe. He knew he was exhausted and maybe not thinking clearly. Surely, he had misunderstood. Confused, Jake made his way into the store.

The young girl behind the counter, who reminded him of Tracey, looked up at him expectantly as he approached the register. "Gas?"

"Yeah. Hey, you know anything about a wedding out at that old house?" Jake fumbled with his wallet.

"Yeah, we were just talking about that." Reaching for the money Jake held out to her, she motioned towards the window with her head.

"Who's getting married?" Jake watched her count the money and press some buttons on the register.

"That Bertrand girl. Her ex was in here earlier today. He was coming get them and bring them home." Handing him the change, she smirked at him. "Honestly, I don't know why she ever left. He's hot."

"What? That doesn't make any sense." Jake shoved the change in his pocket.

"Well, you're a guy. How would you know?" Looking him up and down, her eyes lit up. "Hey, you're the guy. The one everyone is talking about. I love your music. Can I get your autograph?"

"Huh?" Everything seemed to be moving at a different rate of speed around him. She slid a notepad at him. Jake automatically took the pen and wrote his name. His hand felt like someone else's scribbling out the letters. He handed it back, but she had moved from behind the counter. Placing it on the counter, he turned to leave, a strange buzzing in his ears.

"Wait!" The young blonde appeared next to him suddenly, holding out a cell phone over their heads. "Smile." There was a snap and a flash. Jake walked out the door without looking at the picture.

Faith couldn't go back. She said she wasn't going anywhere. Jake had believed her. Not wanting to see anyone, he bypassed the town altogether and took the back roads. The numbness was suffocating. Passing in front of the bar, he decided he was no longer in a hurry to get home. He had spent so much time in this dive, it was like a home away from home anyway. Jake knew this adoptive family would be happy to see the new recording artist with a song on the radio. A lot of good that did him, if the person he wrote the song for was gone again.

Pulling into the gravel parking lot, he thought of his conversation with Amy. She might get her wish. He certainly felt a slew of heart breaking songs just a 'churning in his gut. For now, he would silence it the only way he knew how.

CHAPTER 26

The late afternoon sun streaming through her old bedroom window woke Faith from a deep sleep. She hadn't meant to take a nap, but she was mentally and physically exhausted. She had been busy with a few dessert orders for Easter, and having to pack up the kids. Knowing she wouldn't see them for a whole week had been draining. The surprisingly trying encounter with David earlier had been the last straw. Trying was a pleasant term, but probably not accurate.

The divorce papers had arrived during the week. It was over. She had sat down with Trent and Hannah and explained that her and David were no longer married. They would always be their parents and they loved them, but that at some point they might get remarried to someone else. Trent had become red faced and surly. After some coaxing, Faith finally got to the bottom of it. Ben, one of

Trent's friends on the baseball team, told him that David had spent the night at their house with his mom. Trent thought Ben was lying and told him so. They had a fight. Ben also said that David might be his new dad. After the baseball game, David had taken them all out for pizza. Trent said they acted like boyfriend and girlfriend. Faith reassured him that David still loved him and that nothing would change that. Faith felt sorry for the mom, knowing David, it wouldn't last and after baseball was over, he'd move on.

So she was surprised when David showed up to get the kids and told her to pack a bag. He said he didn't care about the papers, he wanted her to come home. Faith was flabbergasted and didn't know if his performance was for the kids benefit or her parents, but he didn't get to play the victim. She had lost it. Faith hated that her first reaction was to scream at him. Normally she was able to keep a lid on it in front of the kids, but with the stress of the kids leaving for so long and the sadness of the ghost encounters her anxiety had magnified tenfold. Added to the awful way she had let Jake leave, Faith blew up. Even legally divorced, David was still trying to bully her. What pissed her off the most was knowing that he didn't really want her. He was trying to look like the good guy. She was leaving him. She was being unreasonable. Poor David. Faith was sure that sob story went over well with his lady friends. Thankfully, she came to her senses, stopped her ranting and took a deep breath. Then she calmly asked him about Ben's mom, he had become uncomfortable and suddenly in a hurry to be on their way.

After they left, she went to her room and just passed out. Now, she looked around the room where she had spent most of her childhood. Her mother had changed the decor, but it was still her room. She stretched as she got up from the bed and made her way down the hall. She could hear her mother moving around in the kitchen probably preparing the food for tomorrow's feast. Even though she had contributed a few pies herself, she knew her mom was probably busy with some kind of dessert. Faith knew Evan would be more than happy to take any extras home.

Shuffling over the worn linoleum, she entered the kitchen with a yawn.

"Coffee's in the pot. You ok?" Margaret looked up from the mixing bowl.

"Yeah, Mom. I'll be fine. I just hate them being gone for so long." The smell of the coffee cut through the lingering scent of the vinegar from egg dying that morning. Faith had insisted they dye eggs even though they wouldn't be spending Easter with her. It was a tradition she looked forward to every year. She cherished the memories knowing that they would eventually outgrow the excitement of the holidays. Growing up sucked.

"I know, Dear, I was hoping Elle would make it home before they left. They've grown so much since the last time she saw them."

Margaret lined the cookie sheet with parchment paper.

Faith smiled thinking of her little sister and their years of dying eggs and hunting them. Of course, with Faith being nine years older she had overseen the egg dying process until she left for college.

"How long can she stay?" Faith hoped the reunion with her sister would help lessen some of the emptiness of her kids not being there. It would be nice to visit with Elle and hear about her life in Dallas.

"Only a few days. She's got to get back to work."

"Where's Dad?" Faith poured her coffee then leaned on the counter watching her mom spoon out the cookie dough.

"Out in the shop. If you're going out there, tell him to come in when he's hungry. We're just having sandwiches tonight."

Faith wandered outside to her dad's shop following the faint sounds of his radio mixed with the intermittent scream of some kind of saw. The setting sun had turned the sky different shades of orange and pink. The grass was now fully green and little yellow flowers sprouted in patches across the yard. Spring was definitely here.

"What are you doing?" Faith asked her dad when he stopped the grinder.

"Sharpening the blades for my mower. Gotta get that grass cut." He placed the blade carefully on the workbench.

"I thought you were going to let it grow so the kids can hunt eggs." Faith sipped her coffee slowly. She enjoyed the steam from the mug and the warm liquid as she fought the grogginess of her long nap.

"They won't be back for a week. It has time to grow again." He crossed over to the radio and turned it up. "Oh, listen, they gonna play it again."

"Play what?" she asked putting her coffee down on the workbench.

"Your song." He pushed a shop stool in her direction.

The radio announcer was well into his introduction of the next song and she was surprised when she heard Jake's name. Startled, she looked to the radio just as Jake's voice came out of the speaker.

"This song is for Faith. I hope she hears it. I'm sorry I didn't get to play it for you first in person."

Faith squeaked and pulled up the wheeled shop stool to sit. Eyes glued to the radio, she held her breath as she listened. Somewhere in the middle, she remembered to breathe and the tears started. The song was sad and sweet, and she knew at once he hadn't been lying. The melody reminded her of the song she had heard in the dream, or whatever it had been. The words were definitely Jake's. They told of regret and wasted years. When he mentioned the porch, her heart broke. She was flooded with the memories of the ghost couple and was reminded again of the similarities with her and Jake.

> *'Everything that could break down, broke down.*
> *Standin' on the front porch, tryin' not turn around.*
> *She opens the door and my heart says, stand your ground.*
>
> *I see her face and I swear, my future's written right there.*
> *So even if it takes a thousand tries.*
> *I'm gonna see that,*
> *Prairie Cajun Sunrise, in her eyes'.*

The last verse was him telling her he wasn't giving up on them.

"That's a good song he made." Her dad's voice broke through her thoughts. She had forgotten he was there.

"Yeah, Dad. It is." Faith wiped at her eyes and turned to leave. "Mom said to come in when you're hungry."

The shadows had lengthened and merged covering the yard in darkness. Faith walked slowly through the yard, not sure she was ready to go back inside. She needed to talk to him. So deep in her own thoughts she didn't notice Evan and Claire walking over from next door.

Evan called out to her. "Hey, what's going on?"

"Nothing." Faith shook her head still dazed.

"You heard it?" Evan smirked at his sister as they joined Faith.

"Just now." Still a bit overwhelmed, Faith didn't have the words to express what she was feeling.

"It's amazing. I love it!" Claire exclaimed giving Faith a hug.

"I need to talk to him." Faith was still trying to shake off the memories and the guilt of not believing Jake.

"Well, he's back." Evan shrugged. "Go talk to him."

"No, I just heard him talking on the radio in Dad's shop." Faith pointed to the back yard realizing she had left her coffee on the workbench.

"Must have been a recording. That girl at the gas station was showing everybody a picture she took with him when he got back to town today." Evan frowned at his sister.

"Oh."

"He didn't call you?" he asked suspiciously.

"Um, no." Faith smiled at her brother. "I bet he was tired. I'll call him later."

"Did Elle make it here yet? I can't wait to meet her," Claire chimed in changing the subject.

"No, Mom's been waiting all day. She'd said she'd be here before dark," Faith rolled her eyes at the dark sky.

"Did you try and text her to make sure she's ok?" Pulling out his phone, he scrolled through his contacts to message her.

"No, sorry. I've had a rough day, and I'm not thinking clearly."

A few minutes passed and Evan's phone buzzed. Looking at the screen, Evan read the message out loud. "She's fine. Had a stop to make first. Took longer than she thought. Be here in an hour or so."

"Ok, I'll go let mom know so she's not worried." Evan strode off across the yard to relay the message, his long legs making quick work of the small distance.

"Faith, will you talk to him now?" Claire asked as soon as the door shut behind Evan.

"Yeah, I am. I'm going to go over there. Right now."

Faith drove through town, thinking about the song. The lyrics had touched her. It was so Jake. His love for his home showed through, along with the regret for wasting so much time. The line about her being his future just melted her heart. She should have never left Cypress Point or him. She'd had her reasons. It was love plain and simple. She didn't want him and Evan to be at odds. She had come between them, not realizing the damage she had done until it was too late. Then she was afraid for him, so she had let him go.

The back roads brought back those memories, so sweet and hot. They were so young and their hormones had completely taken control. Faith had not considered the consequences of their actions until the reality of what they had done sunk in. It had scared her shitless.

Driving up the long driveway to the farmhouse, she was nervous. She wanted to believe the words he wrote to her. Her hope soared, imagining the future. They were both adults now. There was nothing to stop them from building a life together.

She parked her car behind his truck, glad that he was actually at home. Hearing voices as she approached the door, she hesitated. Not sure if the mumblings were Jake talking to himself or singing maybe. She laughed knocking on the door. The voice sounded again, she assumed it was a muffled 'Come in'.

Faith opened the door, and walked through the living room, making her way to the hallway. She could hear Jake mumbling, and was surprised when a female voice answered him.

"Ugh, I knew we should have taken my car. Do you have any clean clothes?" The voice and the attitude that went with it was familiar.

Faith's insides froze. *Breathe. Breathe.* It couldn't be. This was not happening.

She walked down the hallway and almost ran into the owner of the so familiar voice. Her little sister came out of the bedroom pulling on one of Jake's shirts. It only reached mid-thigh leaving her long tanned legs uncovered.

"Elle?" Not believing what she was seeing, Faith rubbed at her eyes that had begun to sting.

"Faith?" Elle asked in surprise, then rolled her eyes. "Great. Did Mom send you?" Her short spiky hair stood at an odd angle, reminding Faith of Trent first thing in the morning.

"No, Mom did not send me," Faith hissed. "What are you…"

Singing interrupted her question. The mumbling she had heard before was in fact singing. An extremely slurred rendition of Elvis' Little Sister was coming from the bedroom.

"Little sister, don't you. Little sister, don't you. Kiss me once or twice. Tell me that it's nice. Then you run. Little sister, don't you do what your big sister done."

Faith was out the door before he finished.

CHAPTER 27

Faith managed to keep it together long enough to drive out to Serena's. She gripped the steering wheel white knuckled, breathing in through her nose and out through her mouth. She kept her focus on the feeble beams of the headlights splitting the darkness in front of her. She couldn't face her parents or Evan right now. The heaviness in her chest made it hard to breathe and her blood pressure made her head feel like it could explode at any moment. She knew she needed to calm down.

Serena's car was parked in front of the forbidding estate that Faith had come to love. She hoped she could make it to the door. Her dropping dead in the driveway, however unfortunate, would actually be fitting with the sad history of the house. They should change the name to Coeur Mal du Bayou. Could someone die of sadness? Her vision became fuzzy as she fought to open the car door which had suddenly become heavy.

Through blurry eyes Faith watched Serena run out of the house towards her. Serena opened the car door causing Faith to topple out. Serena caught her shoulders and held her up. Faith tried to focus her eyes and barely made out Serena's bare feet under the hem of her colorful skirt. Serena's voice was filled with concern. "What's happening?"

"I can't...talk. I think," Faith gasped desperately for air, "I'm dying." She grabbed at her chest.

"Come inside." Serena reached for her arm.

"I can't." Faith shook her head then grabbed the car door to steady herself.

Serena put an arm around Faith and helped her to the house and into the parlor. Sitting her on the sofa, Serena put a throw around her shoulders. "You're shivering."

"I don't know." Faith pulled the throw closer around her and shut her eyes.

"Tell me." Sitting next to Faith, Serena rubbed her arm.

"I can't. Hurts too much," Faith whispered, a tear rolled down her cheek. "Jake..."

"Breathe, hun. It's going to be ok. Just breathe." Serena got up and moved to a table. Faith heard the strike of a match, and after a few seconds the scent of incense reached her. "Just lie back, and try to relax. Breathe. I'm going to put some tea on."

Eyes still closed, Faith tried to concentrate on breathing. The image of Elle in nothing but Jake's shirt floated before her. No, no, no. Anyone but her. She wanted to rage and lash out, but not at her sister. She wouldn't tear her family apart, but she needed to do something. Faith would never be able to look at her little sister again.

How could he do this? Even if he thought she was still mad at him, this was unforgivable. After making the song for her, and saying he wouldn't give up, to come home and do this. Why? Her brain couldn't wrap around it no matter how hard she tried.

And Elle? What was she thinking? Obviously she didn't know about them. Elle wouldn't have done this if she knew about her and Jake. Elle wouldn't do this to her. Would she? They weren't close, but they were still sisters.

A million thoughts raced through her head. Was that the stop Elle had to make? Jake had said he still talked to her family. Had he and Elle stayed in touch? Oh my God, did they have a relationship at some point over the years?

Before Faith could work herself up again, Serena came into the room. She had pulled her curly black hair back into a loose ponytail at the base of her neck, and watched Faith curiously.

"How did you know something was wrong?" Faith asked trying to take her mind off Elle.

"I can feel them, the spirits." Serena bit her lip and gazed at the ceiling. "Something's not right. This is different." Her dark eyes darted nervously around the room, then stopped on Faith again, "Can you tell me what happened now?"

"Yeah, I heard the song. Jake's song." A few more tears leaked out. "It reminded me of everything, the dream, the ghosts," her voice broke, "the past." Faith let out a sob, "Did you hear it?"

"Yes, actually I did. That's when things started to get weird. I figured it had something to do with you two." Serena sat next to Faith again and patted her hand.

"I went to find him. Evan said he was back." Faith forced herself to take a breath and continue. "I went to his house and he wasn't alone."

Serena sat up in surprise. "Amy?"

"No....not Amy." Faith shook her head, the tears streamed down her face. "My sister, Elle."

"Oh, no. Faith, I'm so sorry." Serena hugged Faith to her.

"She's my sister, and I don't want to ever see her again," Faith sobbed into Serena's shoulder.

Serena held her until the whistle of the kettle sounded from the kitchen. Serena left the room to make the tea, and Faith curled into a ball on the sofa crying into a pillow.

"Here drink this." Serena returned with a cup of tea, placing it on a side table next to the sofa. "I have a feeling it may be a long night."

"I'm sorry. I just can't go home. My kids aren't there, and Elle is." Faith sat back up, wiping her face.

"It's ok, you know you can stay here. I'm just worried." Serena sat across from Faith, her gaze wandering towards the ceiling again.

"Why?" Now that her vision had cleared, Faith noticed how upset Serena was.

"Faith, I've sent a text to Claire, just so they know where you are and that you're ok. Let's just try to stay calm." Rubbing the goosebumps on her bare arms, Serena shivered.

"That's kinda hard right now." Faith reached for the cup on the side table, the air suddenly cold around her.

"It's going to be ok. Drink your tea." Getting up from her chair, Serena lit more incense.

"Serena, you're scaring me." She pulled her hand back, and wrapped the blanket around her again.

"You know how I can feel them? Well, I haven't told y'all everything, but that doesn't matter." She waved her hands and shook her head. "Right now, there's something going on, and the feeling is really strong and really angry. It's going to be a long night," Serena said again this time her dark eyes looked toward the foyer.

"I can't really get too excited about the ghosts right now, they'll have to wait in line," Faith snorted, and picked up her tea.

"Faith, I keep trying to tell you that you and Jake are connected to this."

"I don't understand how." Shrugging under the blanket, Faith sipped her lukewarm tea.

"Have you ever seen a ghost before you came here? Or had any kind of supernatural experience?" Serena's eyebrows raised over her dark eyes.

"No."

"What's happening here isn't a normal haunting..."

A banging at the door made them both jump. Serena rushed to answer it, her skirt swishing as she moved across the floor. Faith held her breath, she couldn't face Jake either.

She heard Evan's voice from the doorway. He sounded annoyed. Faith breathed deeply. Wrapping the throw around her shoulders tighter she got up to see what was going on.

"She's fine. Really, I think she needs some rest, and to stay calm." Serena's voice was firm and she stood in the doorway.

"Look, somebody better tell me what's going on." Her brother's large hand wrapped around the edge of the door. "She never came back. Then we get a text from you saying she's upset but she'll be ok."

"Evan, calm down. She is ok. Maybe you should just go." Serena held the door as if daring him to push it open further.

"Can we just see her?" Claire's worried voice sounded far away.

Faith spoke up from behind Serena, "Serena, it's ok. Evan I'm fine. Just tell Mom I'm staying here tonight."

"What happened?" Evan pushed the door to see Faith better.

A buzzing from his pocket saved Faith from having to answer right away. He looked at the screen and shook his head. "What the hell?"

He looked back up at them narrowing his eyes on Faith. "What happened?"

"Nothing," Faith answered without hesitation. Evan did not need to know about any of this.

"Bullshit! This from Elle. 'Jake won't bring me to my car. He's drunk and looking for Faith. Come get me.'" Walking out onto the porch, Evan pushed the call button and waited for Elle to pick up.

"Where are you?" He growled into the phone. Faith couldn't hear what Elle's answer was, but Evan didn't seem pleased. His nostrils flared and his muscles tensed. "Clothes?" His fingers clenched into a fist, making the veins in his arm bulge.

"I'm here with Faith at Serena's. I'm waiting." Mashing the button, he shoved the phone back into his jeans. "They're on the way here."

"I don't think that's a good idea." Serena shivered looking behind her nervously. "We should go outside."

"Y'all might not want to see this ladies. Better for y'all to wait inside." He nudged Claire towards the door.

"No," Serena's eyes were huge, as she pleaded with Evan, "please, calm down. Your anger is making it worse."

Evan rolled his eyes. "No. I knew this would happen." He pointed a finger at Faith. "You couldn't leave it alone."

A door slammed upstairs.

"Evan, don't." Faith grabbed his arm. "It doesn't matter. Just go, please."

The sobbing started before he could answer. Wide eyed, he looked from Faith to Claire, then to Serena. "What is that?"

"It's her, the ghost." Claire moved away from the door and closer to Evan.

"Please Evan." Serena was pale and shivering.

The truck lights shone on them as it raced up the driveway. As soon as it stopped, Elle jumped out. Still in Jake's shirt, she had added a pair of ridiculously large basketball shorts that hung past her knees. Her purse slung over one shoulder and heels in hand she stormed up to the porch.

"What the hell, Faith?" Elle demanded, her large dark eyes ringed with smudged eyeliner glittered angrily.

"That's what you say to me after what you did with... him?" Faith screamed back pointing in Jake's direction as he stumbled from the truck. "How could you do that?"

"What's it to you? You were always too good for him." Hands on her hips, she taunted her older sister. "Is it true you're going back to that douchebag you were married to?"

Evan stepped off the porch and moved towards Jake.

"No! What are you talking about?" Grabbing at her heart again, Faith forced herself to breathe.

"Everybody's talking about how you're planning a wedding up here at the big house." Elle threw her hands up in the air motioning to the house that towered above them.

"Evan and I are getting married," Claire spoke up her voice soft and unsure.

"Oops! See Jake you drank yourself stupid for nothing." Elle's short hair, still sticking up, pointed in Jake's direction as she jerked her head to look back at him.

"You're not getting married?" Jake had finally made it around the truck.

Evan met him halfway. "You sonofabitch. What are you doing with Elle?"

"Evan, don't be an ass," Jake dismissed Evan, trying to push past him, "I need to talk to Faith."

"No. I think you need to leave, and leave all of my family alone." Evan pushed Jake back towards his truck.

"Make me." Jake pushed back. "You couldn't make me then, and you sure as hell can't now. You had to bully your sister into not seeing me."

Evan landed the first punch, catching Jake off balance. Jake staggered back, rubbing his jaw.

"That's not true." Evan stepped back readying to defend himself. "She came to her senses."

Faith jumped from the porch to stop them. Jake held an arm out to hold her back, anger and confusion playing across his face. Evan took advantage of his distraction, landing a jab to Jake's stomach. Jake went down to his knees. Evan grabbed his shirt and picked him up again. Jake caught Evan around the waist in a bear hug knocking them both to the ground.

The slamming doors and wailing from in the house intensified. Claire and Serena clung to each other overwhelmed by the physical and spiritual violence around them. Faith screamed at Evan to stop. She couldn't be sure if they could hear what she was hearing. The sickening smacks of flesh on flesh and the terrified screams made her dizzy. She grabbed her head and fell to her knees. The screaming continued. Flashes of her father pummeling her lover overwhelmed her.

In a voice not her own, she roared, "No! Poppa, no!"

Faith rushed at Evan pushing him off of Jake. Evan looked up at her. He blinked slowly, the rage leaving his eyes. "Faith?"

"Stop," she sobbed. Turning to Jake, his bloody face was painful to look at.

"What the fuck was that?" Elle asked, her large eyes were glued to the house.

"Elle, not now." Faith helped Jake up from the ground, surveying the damage. His busted lip seemed to be the worst of it, but in the darkness it was hard to tell. She wouldn't be surprised if he was sporting a black eye tomorrow.

"I wrote that song for you Faith. You have to hear it." Still holding his stomach, he pleaded with her.

"And y'all wonder why I don't come home? Another great visit. Evan's getting married. Faith gets a song. And I get puked on. Will someone please take me to my car? I've got to get out of here." Elle gripped the strap of her purse, looking at them expectantly.

"Puked on?" Faith asked turning from Jake to look at her sister.

"Yeah, I stopped to congratulate the big star on his song. He was shitfaced at the bar. The dude asks me to drive him home. Then he throws up on me. I put him in the shower and made him some coffee, but all he kept moaning about was Faith leaving him again. Geesh."

The silence was overwhelming, as if both the humans and spirits were holding their breath.

"You didn't?" Stunned, Faith looked from her sister to Jake.

"Perfect! Yes, thrown up on and now insulted. My family thinks I'm a royal fuck up." Elle stomped her bare foot on the ground, throwing her hands up dramatically.

"Faith, I'd never..." Jake shook his head and winced at the pain. "You have to hear the song."

"I did."

"No, come with me." He held out a hand to her.

"I don't know. I don't think I can do this right now." Faith shook her head, suddenly too tired to argue.

"Faith, please. You have to leave with me right now. I have to take you from this place." Even in the darkness, she could hear the pain and urgency in his voice.

Serena walked up to Faith holding out the throw that had fallen on the ground. "He's right Faith. This is the way it should have ended. She wants you to leave with him. It's too late for her, but it's not too late for you."

Faith took the throw from Serena, and grabbed Jake's hand. Following him to his truck, she thought maybe, just maybe, their story wouldn't end in sadness.

As Faith climbed into the truck next to Jake, she could hear Elle ranting.

"Will somebody please take me to my goddamn car?"

"I'll take you to your car, but then you're going straight to Mom's. She's been waiting all day. And you better watch your mouth, brat."

"Bite me, Evan."

CHAPTER 28

Jake smiled through his cracked lip, not caring that it stung. He could also feel the sore muscles in his gut from Evan's jab. He didn't care about that either. That pain was nothing compared to the awful emptiness he had felt when he thought Faith was going back to David. Reaching out in the darkness across the cab of the truck he felt for Faith's hand.

"I'm sorry Jake." Faith slid her hand into his.

"It's ok, babe. Everything's gonna be ok." Pulling the truck into the overgrown driveway of the old barn, he squeezed her hand reassuringly.

"What are we doing here?" Faith asked.

"This is the only place we've always been able to talk honestly and without interruption. Bring your blanket and grab that flashlight for me." Groaning he got out of the truck and picked up his guitar from the back seat. He was finally going to be able to play the song for her in person. He didn't know why it was so important to him, but he knew she'd understand.

The beam of light bounced around the old barn as Faith looked for a spot to put the blanket down.

Earlier when Elle had told him Faith had come to his house, but that she had ran out, he had almost thrown up again. Knowing she was still there had sobered him up more than the coffee or the shower. He had to see her and stop her from leaving. He practically dragged Elle out of the house to go find her. Elle of course had pitched a fit. She had the Bertrand temperament but was also spoiled. In a hail of curse words and threats, she had finally called Evan. Jake would have went to Serena's eventually, but Elle's temper tantrum had saved him some time. In such a rush to get to Faith, he hadn't thought about what being with Elle looked like to Faith, or Evan for that matter. He wouldn't be making that mistake again he thought, rubbing his sore jaw.

Sitting next to her on the blanket, he pulled the guitar out of the case and began to strum. "Faith, I wrote this song for you after I had the dream."

"I know. I recognized it. It reminds me of the song I heard, too. Pieces of it anyway." Faith closed her eyes as he played.

Jake watching her face closely as he played, could see that she was remembering. When he got to the end, she was in tears. He put the guitar down and held her, "Come here."

"Oh, Jake. I've been so stupid." Faith snuggled into his chest. Jake couldn't help but think of how right it felt.

"No, I don't think so. I was a fool for thinking I had all the time in the world, and for letting you go in the first place. When I heard you were leaving with him today, I thought I was going to die." He stroked her hair, pulling on her ponytail.

"Where did you hear that?" She sat back up to look at him.

"Tracey McMillian and the girl at the gas station."

"That bitch!" Faith's anger put her into motion and she tried to get off the ground.

Jake grabbed her arm pulling her back down to her knees. "I think they just got confused with Evan's wedding but she said that David had been in there and he said he was taking you home."

"Oh no," Faith groaned rolling her eyes as she plopped back down. "He tried to."

"What?"

"He came to pick up the kids and he told me to pack my bags."

"That sonofabitch." His anger flared causing him to clench his fists still sore from his tussle with Evan.

"Jake, you don't have to worry about him. That's over. I got the divorce papers last week. I don't know what got into him, but it's over." Faith rubbed his arm.

"Where was your bodyguard then?" Jake tried to shake off the anger with a joke.

"I'm so sorry about that. Evan..." Faith touched his face softly surveying the damage.

"Is just overprotective. He always has been." Jake finished for her. He couldn't be mad at Evan. If he had a sister, he'd feel the same way.

"I thought he was over that." Frustrated Faith shook her head in the dim light.

"Was he right? I always thought he had bullied you into breaking up with me."

"No, he didn't." Faith lowered her gaze.

"Oh, so you came to your senses?" He couldn't help the sarcasm in his voice.

"No, not like that." Faith patted his chest playfully.

He wanted to kiss her, but he needed some answers once and for all. "Could you please tell me what did happen, so next time I can shut him up?"

"Jake, it was killing me to see what was happening to you and Evan. Y'all had been so close but suddenly y'all were fighting and it was because of me." Her dark eyes pleaded with him for understanding.

"That's it? He would have gotten over it eventually....well, maybe after we had our first kid or something." Jake laughed at his joke. Evan could be so pigheaded it might have taken longer. He could feel Faith tense up in his arms. "Hey I'm joking, but he probably would have come around."

"Umm. There was another reason." She tried to pull away, but he held her still, her eyes large with fear. "I thought I was pregnant and I got really scared."

He let out a breath, then crushed her to him, whispering into her hair. "Oh, Faith, I would have married you in a heartbeat. Why didn't you say something, baby?" Tears stung at his eyes as he thought of a young Faith carrying his baby.

"Because I was terrified for you," she whispered back softly.

"Me?" Jake pulled away to see her face.

"You had just turned 19 and I wasn't even 17 yet. You could have gotten into trouble, and if Evan wouldn't have killed you, my dad would have." A tear rolled down her cheek.

"We would have worked it out." He wiped the tear away. "So you weren't?"

"No, and by the time I figured it out...", she shrugged, "I was just too scared it would happen again." She looked so miserable. He couldn't believe she had gone through that by herself. Knowing she had tortured herself with worry and all the possible outcomes, while he had no clue.

"Hey, I wanted to marry you even back then. Do you remember, I asked you to marry me?" Jake pulled her onto his lap, needing to feel her close to him.

"Yeah, I do, but I didn't think you were serious." Faith smiled at him, wrapping her arms around his neck.

"As a heart attack. So, now we're older. Evan can't kill me, he's a lawman. Ed and I are BFF's."

Faith giggled in his arms. "Is there a question in there somewhere?"

"Hmmm. Yeah. I said I'd wait, but I don't want to. I need to know, it's me and you." Jake gently turned her face to look into her eyes. "And you need to know, there is no one else for me, but you. There never has been."

"So I don't have to worry about Elle?" she teased him.

"The Brat?" Jake rolled his eyes, and laughed. "No, she'll always be your bratty little sister."

Faith smiled at the use of their old nickname for Elle. Careful of his battered lip, she kissed him softly. Ignoring his stinging lip, he kissed her back forcing her mouth open with his tongue. She melted into him, groaning into his mouth. Her hands began roaming over his back.

He pulled back smiling. "Trying to change the subject?"

"Hmmm, no. What were we talking about?" she asked innocently.

The picture Amy had painted in his head came to mind. That's what he had wanted all along. "You're gonna marry me. You and the kids are going to live with me. We are going to sit on the porch, while they play in the yard and I'm going to sing our baby to sleep."

Faith gasped softly, hope shining in her eyes. "Yes. I love you, Jake."

"I love you, too. Should we go? It's getting late, or early." He planted a kiss on her nose then gave her his lopsided grin.

"Mmm. No, I don't think so." Leaving a trail of soft kisses on his cheek, she made her way to his neck. "We used to say we wished we could stay here all night together and watch the sun come up. Now we can." She pushed him back onto the blanket straddling him.

Grinning at her, he reached up and pulled the ponytail holder from her hair. "And I know how we can pass the time."

CHAPTER 29

Faith woke to a dull ache in her hip from the hard ground beneath her. Still wrapped around Jake for warmth she hated to move away from him. The pain in her hip increased forcing her to move.

"Ugh." Trying to sit up made her neck and back join in the protest.

"Hey." Through half open eyes Jake watched her. "It's morning."

The rising sun seemed to be chasing away the gray and coloring the sky beautiful shades of pink and yellow. Faith breathed in the fresh air and shivered a bit. Looking for her clothes, she groaned again, "Ugh. What was I thinking?"

"What's wrong? You don't like sleeping on the ground?" Jake offered her shirt to her, and she snatched it from him hurrying to put it on.

"No. That's why I had Evan camp out with Trent. Everything hurts and I look like I've been rolling around in the dirt." Faith motioned to the small blanket that had bunched up underneath them during the night leaving their legs in the dirt.

"We were rolling in the dirt. At least you had a pillow." Jake tried to lift the arm she had been laying on and winced. "Oh, yeah, and you don't have a hangover or get an ass kickin' last night." He held his stomach and let out a groan forcing himself to sit up. Faith couldn't help but admire the sight of him, even hurt. She wanted to take care of him, kiss all the pain away and make up for all the lost time. Knowing she would have the chance to, made up for any discomfort she was feeling at the moment.

"Hey, last night..." Trying to find the words, Faith hesitated.

"What?" Those warm chocolate eyes watched her expectantly as he pulled his jeans over his legs.

"You meant what you said. I know that. So did I, Jake..." She didn't want to be parted from him for any reason, but her kids had to come first.

"But?" His hands stilled on his waistband and she could see the dread on his face.

"My kids."

"They'll need time to get used to me being around. I get that." Nodding his head slowly, he finished buttoning his jeans. "Just promise me, you'll always answer me, even if it's just a text. You have to talk to me, Faith."

"Yes, I promise." Faith pulled on her jeans relieved. The thought of her phone had her feeling the pockets of her jeans. "Oh, my phone." She looked around frantically. "It must be at Serena's. Can you bring me over there first?"

"Yeah, but I'm not leaving you there." Snapping the latches shut on his guitar case, he looked up at her his face determined.

"Jake, you do realize I work there?" She turned from him to snatch up the flashlight, clicking it off.

"Yeah, but.." He stood ready to argue, pulling his shirt over his head.

"I don't think we have to worry about that anymore. I left with you last night. Maybe we broke the cycle." Faith handed him the flashlight.

"Cycle?"

"She's been reliving those traumatic experiences. Losing her lover and her baby." Suddenly sad, Faith looked down realizing she had put a hand over her stomach. "I guess that's why she chose us."

"Oh, wow. Me, you and the baby. Evan wanting to kill me." He clicked the flashlight on and off as he thought it over, "Do they know about the baby?"

"There was no baby, and no, they don't know." Pulling her hands away from her stomach, she gave him a worried look.

"Fine by me. I'm not looking for another fight." Jake rolled his shoulders and turned to pick up his guitar case.

"So where to first?"

"What do you mean?" Jake started walking towards the truck.

"You don't want to leave me at Serena's, so we'll go to your house first. You can get cleancd up. Then you can bring me to Serena's to get my car and follow me home."

"Home?" Putting the case down, he turned back towards her.

"Easter Sunday dinner at my parents'." Faith pointed to the sunlight now streaming through the cracks of the old barn.

"Really?" His lopsided grin melted her heart and the love in his eyes gave her hope for a happily ever after.

"Yeah. Don't worry, Mom won't let Evan or Elle make a scene in front of company." Laughing she picked up the blanket and shook it out.

Jake's laugh filled the barn. Pulling his phone out of his pocket, he held it up. "Hey, take a picture with me."

"Right now?" Faith pushed the hair from her face, frowning at him.

"Yeah." He pulled her close and held the phone up over their heads. "Later, too. I want lots of pictures of us together."

His unexpected request, made her laugh. Faith looked up into the screen, and was overwhelmed by the sight of them together. Even with his busted lip, and her loose tousled hair, they were the picture of happiness.

Breathe. Breathe. There was nothing to be nervous about. Faith could feel the familiar jittering in her stomach as they pulled into her parents driveway. Serena had let her take a shower and borrow a colorful sundress while Jake had waited nervously in the parlor. Now she was the one fidgeting nervously and she didn't know why. Evan, Claire and Elle knew about her and Jake. She was sure her dad had a pretty good idea about them too after hearing the song Jake had written for her.

Jake squeezed her hand, and nodded towards the house. "You ok?"

"Yeah." Opening the truck door, she was glad he had insisted on them taking his truck together.

Evan and Claire drove up right behind them. Claire jumped from the truck, her blue eyes shining. "We have puppies!" She ran to Faith and hugged her forcefully. "Three!"

Evan approached giving Jake a dark look. Noticing his split lip he gave a little smirk, then offered his hand. "Sorry, man."

Jake shook his hand, "It's alright, looks like I got one in, too." He pointed to a cut on Evan's cheek bone.

"Yeah, whatever." Evan pushed Jake's hand away.

"Y'all come on in. Foods ready," Margaret called from the porch.

As they filed into the kitchen, Ed watched them curiously from his seat at the table.

"It's about time y'all got here," Elle pouted from the living room. She entered the kitchen, and Faith was surprised to see her hair still sticking up. In the light she could see the tips were a bright red.

"Is your hair supposed to look like that?" Faith blurted out.

Elle snorted and rolled her huge eyes at Faith. "Yes."

"Jake, I'm so glad you came. What a nice surprise!" Margaret beamed at him guiding him towards the table.

"That's a good song you made," her father spoke up from his chair at the table.

Jake grinned outstretching a hand to Faith's father. "Thanks, Ed! I hope I'm not intruding." Seeing Jake and her father shake hands, Faith blew out a breath.

"Not at all. It's been too long." Margaret patted him on the shoulder and smiled at Faith. She had worried for nothing. Her mother would never make anyone feel unwelcome.

They all sat at the table and looked at each other uncomfortably.

"So are we just not going to talk about last night?" Elle asked incredulously.

"Elleanor Grace," Margaret warned from the stove.

"Mom, I know you saw their faces. Aren't you going to ask?" She drummed her fingers on the table, glaring at Evan.

"Hmm. You come home and started trouble girl?" Ed asked Elle gruffly.

"What?" Elle slapped her hands on the table. "I'm the trouble maker? They fought last night. Each other." She wagged a finger from Evan to Jake and back again.

"Looks like they got it straightened out." Nodding towards his wife Ed added, "Don't upset your mother."

"I can't help it if she doesn't like my hair, Dad," Elle muttered under her breath.

Evan smirked at Elle, then turned to Faith. "Speaking of hair, where's your ponytail, Sis?"

Faith smiled at him narrowing her eyes. "I thought I'd wear it down today."

Jake put an arm around her shoulders and squeezed. Leaning over he whispered in her ear, "I'll buy you some new ponytail holders."

"It looks lovely Dear." Margaret placed a bowl of potatoes on the table. "And I don't think I've seen that dress before."

Elle let out a groan from across the table.

"It's Serena's. She let me borrow it. Here let me help." Faith got up to help set the food out. There'd be less talk with the food to keep their mouths busy.

"Why didn't she come?" Her mother handed her the green bean casserole. "I don't think it's good that she keeps herself up there in that house all alone."

"I asked her Mom. She didn't want to, but I told her I'd bring her some food back." Placing the bowl on the table, Faith thought of her friend. Serena had seemed fine this morning. Maybe it was over.

"Oooh. I want to go." Elle sat up straighter, excitement shone in her brown eyes. "Claire told me she reads cards and I want her to read mine."

"I can ask her for you. If you want." Claire smiled at Elle.

"Thanks. I wonder if we'll hear the ghost again. That was so freaky." The expression on Elle's face along with the spiky hair cut made her look even younger than she was. "Gah, I should have got it on video." She smacked herself on the forehead.

"Elleanor," Evan growled.

"Don't call me that, Evan." Elle slapped at his arm.

"Ok, brat." Rubbing his hand through her spiky hair, he laughed.

"That's enough," Ed grumbled a warning.

"Rosie had her puppies last night," Claire offered awkwardly.

Faith smiled at Claire. "I'm sorry the kids weren't here. They'll be excited."

"They'll have their pick, when they get back." Evan grinned at her.

"Oh, no, you don't." Faith pointed a finger at Evan then grabbed a stack of plates.

"Aww, come on, babe. Kids should have a dog." Taking a plate from her, Jake winked at Faith.

"So you two are back together?" Elle asked biting her lip, looking at Faith.

"Yeah, we are," Jake answered before Faith could open her mouth.

"Anything else you need cleared up?" Faith leaned over Elle putting a plate on the table in front of her with a smack.

"Yeah," Elle rolled her eyes. "Do I get to be in your wedding, too?"

"Too?" Faith blinked in surprise.

"Claire asked me to be in her wedding." Elle smiled sweetly batting her eyelashes.

"I said only if you fix your hair," Evan teased as he took two plates from Faith putting one in front of Claire.

"Let's get Claire and Evan married first. Then we'll talk." Faith heard her mother sniff from the sink.

"Are we gonna eat today?" Ed growled but the smile on his face let them know it was all show.

"Yeah, Dad. Here." Faith handed him a plate. "I think that's everything. Mom come sit."

Faith traded glances with her siblings amid the passing and sharing of food, and they all grinned at each other. Those smiles held a wealth of shared memories that made them family. She could feel the stress of these past months finally begin to fade. It was good to be home.

Elle pulled up to the gas pumps, thinking about the last few days. This visit had been different, with everyone there it had felt like home again. She hated to leave without seeing her niece and nephew, but she'd be back soon. Evan and Claire's engagement party was next month and she had no intention of missing it.

After filling the tank, she decided to grab a drink for the road. Her combat boots scraped against the warm asphalt of the parking lot as she walked. A stray breeze blew the skirt of her sundress around her legs threatening to lift it. Her black tipped fingers held it in place as she reached for the door. The electronic beep of the door brought a sudden halt to the conversation of a group of young girls inside.

The blonde behind the counter gave Elle a curious glance, obviously taking in her hair and dress. Elle supposed it wasn't a typical style out here in Hooterville which was one of the reasons she left Cypress Point as soon as she was able.

She pushed her sunglasses on top of her spiky hair, giving the cashier her usual combination of a smirk and eye roll then headed to the coolers. As soon as she was out of sight, the conversation started up again.

"He's so hot."

"Yeah, I know. He comes in here all the time. He and my mom have a thing."

Elle listened as she perused the case of cold drinks.

"Really? That's awesome. Are they a couple?"

"No, it's not serious."

"Yeah, I guess not. He's a musician, so I'm sure he's got a lot of women wantin' to get with him. But your mom can say she slept with Jake Fusilier."

Elle's hand froze in midair halfway into the cooler. Remembering Jake's drunken ramblings a few nights ago, she connected the source of his false information. Another reason she ran from Cypress Point, small town gossips. Grabbing a drink, she let the cooler door shut on its own and made her way to the counter.

As she approached, she gave the cashier a friendly smile. "I couldn't help but overhear. You know Jake Fusilier?"

"Yeah," she answered proudly.

One of her friends, not wanting to be left out, boasted, "She has a picture with him on her cell phone."

"Wow! Really? Can I see it?" Elle widened her eyes in awe.

The cute blonde cashier, whose name tag said Jade, pulled her phone from her pocket and quickly scrolled to find her prized picture. She handed the phone to Elle then turned to ring up her drink.

"Ahhh. This is awesome." Elle held the phone up in front of her as she quickly pressed delete. Then she gave a wicked smile into the camera while she help up her middle finger.

"That's great." Elle slid the phone back across the counter with her credit card. "You'd better hang on to that. That guy is going to be famous one day."

Jade handed her card back, blushing.

Elle smiled sweetly and waved. "Y'all have a great day!"

'Too Bad,' she thought to herself as she walked back to her car, *'I won't be around to see the show.'* She smiled into the wind, not caring if her dress blew up. They could kiss her ass.

CHAPTER 30

Everything had to be perfect. It was the first official event at Coeur du Bayou. Even though it wasn't a huge event, Faith wanted everything to go smoothly. It was a trial run for bigger things to come. She and Serena had talked Evan and Claire into having an engagement party to celebrate their upcoming marriage. They hadn't wanted a big to-do, but settled on an intimate dinner party for family. It gave them a perfect opportunity to set the stage, the table and the mood.

Faith had been working nonstop between her shifts at the diner, baking, planning the menu and the cake. From her spot in the foyer, she glanced through the open double sliding doors into the big room, where the photographer was taking pictures. Serena had hired a friend of hers, so they would have pictures to show new clients. He was busy snapping away at the cake table. She smiled with pride at the sight of her creation. Two small tiers of cake decorated with ruffles of cream, gold, mint and violet, and topped with handmade flowers of pink and purple. Nestled next to the flowers lay a small open ring box holding a gum paste ring with a clear candy diamond.

"They're here!" Hannah danced excitedly in front of the sidelight. "Can we go meet them?"

"At the door. Don't either one of you take a step off of that porch," Faith warned. Keeping her kids clean and their clothes straight while they waited for everyone to get there hadn't been an easy task.

Trent pulled open the heavy wooden door for his grandparents.

"I'm just saying they need to change the date of the wedding..." Ed frowned at his wife.

"Shhhh." Margaret held up a hand to quiet her husband then greeted Faith with a smile. "Everything is so beautiful, Dear." She looked around the foyer and peeked into the parlor, her eyes shining.

"Mom." Faith tried to get her mother's attention. "It's in here."

"Ohhh." Margaret sighed with appreciation at the sight before her. "It's beautiful! Oh, Faith, everything is beautiful!"

Faith laughed. "Thanks Mom. It's mostly Serena's doing, but the cake was me."

Her mother wandered into the room to get a closer look at the cake.

"Why do they need to change the date of the wedding?" Faith asked turning to her father.

"What? We're not changing the date," Evan spoke from the doorway.

"I'm just saying, you two, and a wedding in October.....you're asking for a hurricane." Her father pointed out to the gloomy sky through the open front door.

Evan put his head down at his father's suggestion. Faith knew he was referring to the night Claire and Evan met, and the bigger storm that occurred on Halloween night.

"Dad." Faith rolled her eyes, but looked back towards the open door at the dangerous fast moving clouds that appeared suddenly. Trent was at the edge of the porch to greet Claire's parents. "Let's not talk about it now."

Evan greeted his soon to be in laws, and escorted them to their seats. Trent and her father followed them in, both looking uncomfortable in their dress clothes. Faith watched with amusement as the three of them all tugged at the collars of their stiff shirts.

A gust of wind blew in through the door and in walked Elle. Decked out in a slim fitting maxi dress that showed off her slight build. The dangerously high slit in the side showed off her long legs as she moved. The black dress decorated with bright red poppies highlighted the red tips of her spiky hair and a small diamond stud glinted from her left nostril.

"That's new." Faith pointed out the nose ring in shock.

"Oh, yeah." Elle reached up touching the stud absently. "I've got to give you losers something to talk about."

"Are you trying to kill Mom and give Dad a stroke?" Faith frowned at her little sister.

"No, Mom just doesn't understand and Dad...well, he doesn't care." Elle shrugged looking around.

"Is that what you think?"

"Whatever. Who is that?" Elle motioned towards the room where Gil had popped in to fill the water glasses. He cleaned up well. In dress clothes and an unstained crisp white apron, he made quite a picture.

"Gil?" Faith giggled at the expression on her sister's face.

"It can't be. That geek that used to follow you around in high school?" The grimace on Elle's face was comical.

"Yes, be nice."

"You're no fun." Her big brown eyes surveyed the room. "Where's Claire?"

"She's upstairs getting ready." Faith glanced nervously up the staircase.

"Oh, can I go up? I want to look around." Elle's gaze followed the massive staircase up to the landing above in awe.

"Maybe later. Hannah, show Aunt Elle to her seat, please."

Hannah shyly reached for her aunt's hand, and blushed prettily as they made their way into the room. Faith watched for Evan's reaction to the nose ring.

She was startled when strong arms wrapped around her waist from behind, pulling her into the foyer and out of the doorway. She recognized those arms and smiled. Those arms were home.

"Damn, woman, what do you have on?" Jake ran his hands over her hips when she turned to face him. Her dress, a mint green snug fitting pencil dress with a floral print, had been the inspiration for the cake.

"And where is your ponytail?" His eyes roamed appreciatively up to her face slowly.

"Don't you like my hair?" Faith tried to step back but the wall was behind her. Her hand went to her hair, gingerly patting the pins that held it all up.

"Yeah, I do. I'm not going to be able to keep my hands off of you. Maybe we can sneak upstairs later." He gave her that lopsided grin and she melted.

"The kids are here," she reminded him, "But I can send them home with my parents. I'll need to help clean up."

"Beautiful and smart." He leaned in to kiss her, and she met him halfway. Their lips touched sending a tingle through her. She wrapped her arms around him, forgetting where they were.

A flash went off interrupting their kiss. *Snap. Snap.*

"Wha..." Jake blinked into the camera.

"It's ok. This is Ben, a friend of Serena's. He's a photographer, here to take pictures of everything for us."

"Oh....great!" He smiled at the young man with the camera. "Hey, take a picture of us. Just us. Then later we can get one with the kids."

Over the last month, Jake had started visiting with her dad at first, helping him in the shop with whatever needed to be done. Trent had taken to him instantly, following him around asking question after question. Hannah simply adored him and constantly begged him to sing for her. Any reservations she had were long gone.

The photographer suggested they stay with their arms around each other, but turn just their faces towards the camera. Locked in his arms, she smiled. The happiness, love and hope she felt shone in her eyes as the camera flashed.

Jake took the opportunity to kiss her neck making her smile widen. Snap, the camera flashed again.

He began to sing softly in her ear, "I gotta have Faith...Faith...Faith."

She threw her head back laughing heartily. *Snap. Snap. Snap.*

"What the hell? I thought Claire had come down with all that flashing." Evan frowned at them from the doorway.

A door slammed shut upstairs, and they all turned at the sound to gaze up the stairs. Evan froze. Faith heard the whoosh of air as he let out a breath. Claire, as gorgeous as any fairy tale princess, stood on the landing smiling down at them. Her dress of deep purple jersey, clung to her ample curves bringing out her fair skin and blue eyes. Serena appeared next to her and they made their way down the stairs.

Faith looked back to her brother, who was now grinning from ear to ear.

"Don't just stand there, Brother Dear." Faith gave him a push.

"What was I waiting for again? I don't remember." Evan gave her a wink, and walked to the bottom of the stairs to wait for Claire.

"The next time you wait for me to come down these stairs, I'll be in white." Claire reached for Evan's hand, her blue eyes twinkling.

"I can't wait, Darlin'."

Snap. Snap. Snap.

"Oh, now, he's in a hurry," Faith snorted behind them, rolling her eyes. She watched them enter the big room then turned back to Serena, who had a death grip on the newel post.

"Serena, what's wrong?"

"Nothing." Serena shook her head and took a step off the stairs. "Y'all go on in. I'll go make sure everything is ready to serve."

"I can do that. You've done everything else."

"No, it's your family. You should be with them. Go enjoy yourselves." Serena pushed them towards the open double doors.

Jake took Faith's hand and lead her to the table to find their seats.

The meal was delicious, even if Faith said so herself. She couldn't take all the credit. Gil had helped and the presentation was Serena's doing. She had no doubt this endeavor would be successful. Serena had definitely set the mood for an elegant dinner party. White linen table cloths with crisp folded napkins, fancy silverware and classic white china adorned the tables. Candles holders of various heights mixed in with the spring bouquets of the tablescape added to the ambiance.

Faith smiled as the photographer took a few more shots then wandered over to Serena. Serena had introduced him as an old acquaintance, but their constant whisperings and knowing looks had Faith curious. She watched them now, their conversation intense. Several times throughout the meal Faith thought she had caught a whiff of incense, and Serena had flitted around nervously. Something was definitely up. Faith had thought the ghostly episodes were over. Serena never mentioned anything, but watching her now she wasn't so sure.

When the meal was over, they posed for a few more family pictures. Faith sent the kids home with her parents and started the cleanup. Claire and Evan walked out with her parents to say goodnight. Noticing the rain, Faith smirked to herself. She could about imagine the conversation her parents were having.

Serena stood in the foyer waiting for everyone to leave. Jake, having his own reason to hurry along the process, offered to help clear the dishes. When he carried off a stack to the kitchen, Faith went to the foyer to meet Serena. "What's going on?"

Serena sent a glance to the photographer before answering. "Nothing. Everything's fine."

"What can we do to help?" Evan pulled off his tie as soon as the door shut behind him and Claire.

"No, y'all should go on home. It was your party." Serena smiled at them warmly.

"Really?" He raised a dark brow at Serena then looked to Claire.

"We've got this. Take Claire home."

"Ok, let me run upstairs to get my stuff." Claire slipped off her heels to hurry up the stairs.

"How come you're sending them home?" Faith asked suspiciously.

"I can take care of it. You've done so much. Actually, maybe you should send Gil and his helpers home, too." Serena anxiously watched Claire climb the stairs.

"I'm not leaving you with this mess."

Jake came out of the kitchen with his sleeves rolled up. "Ok, the tables are cleared and the girls have started washing. Want me to pick up the tablecloths and put the candles out?" he asked Serena.

"No, I'll get that," she answered blocking the doorway.

"Serena, is everything ok?" Evan glanced suspiciously from Serena to the photographer.

"Of course."

A door slammed upstairs, and Serena jumped. Claire appeared on the landing.

"Oh, Claire," Serena cried and held a hand out in warning.

"What?" Claire stopped on the first step.

"Be careful...It's Richie," Serena hissed, her dark eyes looking past Claire.

"Where?" Gripping the railing, her blue eyes widened in fear, the color draining from her face.

"Behind you."

The photographer's camera went off in a hail of flashes.

"Cut it out, man," Evan growled at him. When Claire didn't move, Evan spoke softly to her. "Darlin', come on down."

A thunderclap shook the house, the electricity blinked off freezing everyone in place. It blinked again, and in the instant between light and dark, the figure of a man standing behind Claire on the stairs generated a collective gasp from the onlookers. Then the electricity went out completely leaving them in darkness except for the candles in the big room. Faith moved toward the candlelight trying not to panic. *Breathe. Breathe.* Jake grabbed her hand in the darkness.

"Claire don't move. I'll get a candle." Serena hurried into the big room. The soft glow of light grew as she made her way back into the foyer with a candle.

Suddenly, the massive front door of Coeur du Bayou opened, letting in a violent gust of wind and making the candle flame dance wildly. The flickering light revealed the grimace of surprise on Serena's face as she gaped at the open doorway.

A shadowy figure stood on the threshold. A deep voice exploded over the driving rain outside.

"Rena? Have you lost your mind? What are all these people doing here?"

"Who the hell are you?" Evan stepped in front of Serena protectively.

"I'm her husband. Who the hell are you?"

Prairie Cajun Sunrise

Everything that could go wrong, went wrong.
Gave me everything I needed, to write this song.
Drivin' into the sun, on a warm Louisiana dawn.

Was it something I said? Is someone else in my bed?
Wish I could take back all them lies, with that,
Prairie Cajun Sunrise in my eyes.

Everything that could go bad, went bad.
Pissed away the best thing, that I ever had.
Drivin' home to set it right, with my heart in my hand.

Sometimes 'sorry' won't do, 'cause love can see right through,
even the best disguise. When that,
Prairie Cajun Sunrise is in your eyes.

Maybe I've gone too far? Get myself on back to the bar.
Spend another night drinkin' with the guys, but then that
Prairie Cajun Sunrise is in my eyes.

Everything that could break down, broke down.
Standin' on the front porch, tryin' not turn around.
She opens the door and my heart says, stand your ground.

I see her face and I swear, my future's written right there.
So even if it takes a thousand tries. I'm gonna see that,
Prairie Cajun Sunrise… in her eyes.

© 2004 Words & Music - Dwayne A Coots
Available as a free MP3 download for readers of this book:

Visit: lisacoots.com/books/hope/pcs

A Word from the Author

As I was finishing the ending of the first book, Promise, the characters of this book were restless. Faith and Jake wanted to tell me their story. I had to quiet them to finish the book. Once I started writing book two, Hope, they led me through the story and I was pleasantly surprised. Now, as I'm finishing this story, the characters from book three are not as loud, but they are whispering to me. The release date for Magic, Book Three of the Trilogy is tentatively set for December 2015.

On the other hand, Elle is stomping her foot, impatiently waiting for her turn. Look for her story in 2016.

ABOUT THE AUTHOR

Lisa Coots grew up in the tiny Louisiana village of Lacassine, but has always yearned for the challenge of a new adventure. Her youthful dreams ranged from the artistic: as a sketch artist and painter; to the studious: as a writer and librarian.

Lisa's dreams were nudged aside, as dreams often are, by conventional reality. Marriage and motherhood came easily to her and she successfully raised three remarkable children and an amazing husband. When the first pangs of empty nest syndrome came a rapping, she eagerly returned to the artistic passions of her youth; painting, designing, and of course, writing.

Lisa Coots now lives in a slightly larger village in Louisiana with her loving family and lots of furry friends.

LisaCoots.com